DREAMING THE PERPETUAL DREAM

DREAMING THE PERPETUAL DREAM

J.K. NORRY

Dreaming the Perpetual Dream

ISBN-13: 978-1-944916-70-1

Suddden Insight Publishing
Indie publishing for the Indie Author
www.suddeninsightpublishing.com

For the dreamer...

ONE

Magazines lined the tabletop, the covers speaking their contents in airbrushed photos and catchy headlines. Worn corners and ruffled pages were a strong deterrent against any curiosity the images might evoke, considering their location. All of the seats were fabric, which made it as uncomfortable to sit in them as it would have been to leaf through a gossip or garden periodical.

Link almost chuckled under his breath at the thought of standing in a corner and avoiding physical contact with everyone in the room like he was already avoiding eye contact with them. It only made sense, in a room made to cycle sick people through it; but only Link seemed to be conscious of it. Without looking, he watched half the waiting patients leaf through magazines while he watched the other half touch themselves and then their seats.

All he could do was his very best to lose himself in his phone. No messages awaited to grab his attention, and no game existed that was compelling enough to evaporate his time. It seemed unfair to him, to have such a myriad of ways to communicate and yet feel more awkward than ever all at the same time. With different ways to text and email and post on every forum, the only real assurance he had was that none of what he did worked to get him what he wanted.

Lost as he was in his thoughts, it took a couple of repetitions of his name before Link heard it. Someone had stood in the doorway so many times since he had sat down, and called out some name other than his, that the first reaction he had was to ignore it.

"Nash," the voice came, for the third or fourth time, "Lincoln Nash."

Link sat up, blacked out the screen on his phone without shutting down the window. He waved his hand, even as he felt a flush creeping up the back of his neck.

"Oh, hey," he said, rising and teetering at the same time. "That's me."

She had already turned away, giving him a scant second to catch the door before it swung shut on its own behind her. Link shouldered his way through, and followed her to a small empty room.

"Have a seat, Mister Nash," she said, halfway in another doorway.

She hesitated, and smiled, so he smiled back.

"My friends call me Link," he volunteered.

Her smile fell.

"Of course, Mister Nash," she said politely. "The doctor will see you soon."

She closed the door, rather abruptly.

There were no new messages on his phone, no matter how many windows he opened. Link had time to check them all several times before the door opened again, time to consider and reconsider washing his hands in the stainless sink, and a few more minutes to sit and be alone.

"Lincoln," floated in front of the doctor, as the door opened. It was followed by a clipboard, then a stethoscope; a body came behind it all.

Link nodded, and smiled.

Close enough.

"Hi," he said, to reply somehow.

"It's been awhile."

The clipboard came down, and Link was nodding.

"I know," he shrugged. "I've been fine."

"Was I the doctor here, last time you visited?"

Trying to smile, he shook his head.

"No," he said. "I wasn't going to say anything because I honestly don't remember his name. I do remember that he was older than you, and definitely not female."

Her smile was automatic, and looked a little forced.

"Does that bother you?" she asked.

Link shrugged.

"My insurance picks my doctor," he replied. "If I got to pick, I would probably choose a female if I chose based on gender. Women tend to be more detail-oriented and capable of multi-tasking, as well as being smarter on average. Honestly, I'm happy to see the change."

For a long moment it looked as though she was looking for something to find offensive in what he had said. Link found his own mind going back over it, after marveling that he had been able to successfully string a sentence together in front of a total stranger.

Following a considered pause, she nodded. She glanced at her clipboard, and spoke while looking at it.

"So, Mister Nash," she said. "What seems to be the problem?"

Her decision to avoid eye contact with him left Link feeling a lot more alone with his thoughts. Grateful for her decision, he collected them.

"I guess..." he began, only to finish lamely.

"Sleep?" he shrugged.

Her eyes left the clipboard, to find his wandering the room.

"You can't sleep?" she said. "I hope you aren't looking for a prescription to knock you out at night. I will write prescriptions, but only when I feel it is absolutely necessary. I'm not that kind of doctor."

His eyebrow arched higher the more impassioned her speech became, and he nodded when it seemed like she was done.

"Okay," he said. "I'm not looking for a prescription, though; and I'm not trying to sleep more. I'm trying to sleep less."

Link could tell that she was trying not to laugh at him, and she bit her lower lip to keep it from spilling out.

"How much do you sleep, on average?" she asked.

He took a moment to think about it, as if he hadn't been thinking of nothing else for so long that it actually drove him to schedule an appointment with a doctor.

"Seven or eight hours a night," he said. "I know, it's normal; but I want to sleep more."

Their eyes met then, and Link wondered if she had taken that wrong.

"I mean, I don't want to," he clarified. "I feel like I want to. There's no desire to get out of bed, but there is a lot of desire to just go back to sleep."

Giving herself time to think, the doctor turned slowly to set the clipboard down. When she turned back to him, she seemed to be wearing a practiced look of genuine concern. Link wondered if it was genuine, or practiced, or both.

"Have you tried giving in?" The look was still there, even as she spoke in a mildly condescending tone. "Maybe if you sleep a little more for a couple days, you'll get caught up. That could be all you need."

The list of things he had tried were likely to be pretty

close to her list of suggestions, but he knew she had to go through them.

"Yeah," Link said. "I slept eighteen hours a day, two weekends in a row. I didn't feel any more or less tired after, just like I wanted to sleep even more."

She was nodding as he spoke, ready to hit the next item on the list.

"Has anything happened lately?" she went on. "A death in the family, a breakup, a job loss?"

The temptation to explode was not a strong one, but it was there. Link wanted to shout that he had exhausted all of the common things, and that the internet had provided the same list for him to check off. That's why he was here, for some secret knowledge that might be worth seeking. It was also why he hadn't been to see a doctor for so long; the easy stuff was easy.

Link forced a laugh.

"I'm no more depressed than anyone else," he said. "I have a good job and all that, and no one close to me has died or walked away lately. I just find sleep more interesting than being awake."

The words hit his ears at the same time as they did hers, and he added a touch more commentary.

"Lame, right?"

She was looking away again, perhaps regretting her decision to shed the shielded safety of the clipboard.

"Of course not," she said. "You are depressed, then? Are you taking something for that? You may not know this, but SSRIs are pretty notorious for causing disturbances in the sleep cycle."

"I'm not taking anything," Link shrugged. "You're not that kind of doctor, I'm not that kind of patient. I believe that most depression is there to be examined, not ignored or medicated. A good dose of unhappiness is often required to propel us towards greater happiness. I know that. I know that some foods cause sleep disturbances, and that lots of medications cause nightmares. I don't take any drugs, and I've tried altering my diet in every way I could think of."

The doctor was looking at him again, pregnant with some comment that was obviously bursting to be given voice. Her eyes had been glazed with the look for more than half of what he said, and Link was afraid she was about to suggest that he alter his diet.

"Do you dream?" she asked, instead.

Several seconds passed while he filtered his words through his thinking process, and Link realized that none had made it through at all. He studied a poster behind her, a drawing of a man and woman facing each other; they were missing both clothing and the half of their bodies that had been sliced off to make the diagram. Still, they were both slightly smiling.

"Sure," Link said. "Everyone dreams, right?"

"Nightmares?"

"Nah." Link waved his hand, dismissively. "Just dreams."

Either she was picking up on his discomfort or she had an idea she needed to chase down; whichever it was, she pressed him further.

"Nothing special about your dreams?" she said. "At all?"

The two half people were of no help, spilling their guts with smiles on their faces. Link shrugged again.

"I guess," he said. "I kind of have lucid dreams, I suppose. I've had them since I was a kid, and didn't know they were unusual until I started looking into sleep disorders. I say 'kind of' because I'm not always in control. I do always know I'm dreaming, even when I get the sense that what is happening is..."

Link trailed off, pretended to be particularly interested in the bloodless gory print on the wall.

"Lucid dreams," she echoed. "You know that you're dreaming, but you still somehow feel that the dream is real?"

They practiced for awhile not looking at each other, and she picked up the clipboard while he let his eyes roam the environment. He mused that it was a room made to give the impression of sterility, and also the most likely place that a person might get sick.

She was writing something.

"Sometimes people come to me for a prescription," she said, "usually for some kind of anti-depressant. Generally I tell them to start working out, or eating better. Every once in a while, I do this."

In one smooth and apparently practiced motion, she ripped a sheet from her clipboard and handed it to him.

"Take one of these when you first wake up," she said. "Come back and see me in four to six weeks, and let me know how it's working."

Link eyed the paper, not surprised that he could not read a word of what she had written.

"What is it?"

She smiled, relieved that she had found a solution.

"It's a generic version of a popular narcolepsy treatment," she said, still smiling. "It has been shown to have benefits for all kinds of sleep conditions, and I'm pretty confident it will help with yours as well."

Link took the slip from her, folded it and put it in his pocket.

TWO

The fact that it was Saturday should not have any bearing on whether or not he took a pill. They had worked so well Thursday and Friday, and a month's prescription didn't take weekends off. Just because he had no plans and no desire to make any didn't mean he shouldn't get his brain in waking mode.

Waking mode…that's how he had come to lovingly refer to his time on the pills, in his mind. It was almost as if Link had lived his whole life with an extra set of eyelids, and didn't realize they were there. A few minutes after swallowing the first one, that first morning, those eyelids had peeled back suddenly. Without any effort or intention to do so, Link was staring at a new world by the time he splashed water on his face. He had felt the eyelids close, slowly, as the hours passed; they were flung open the next morning by another pill, and he was delightfully immersed in waking mode again.

Now there was nothing to do, and a pill assigned to help him do it. Link took one, with a sip of the bottled water on his nightstand, and lay back in bed again. He didn't have to wait long to feel its effects, but that didn't mean he couldn't continue to lie there awhile longer.

When sleep became a favorite hobby, Link had decided that some nicer sheets might be in order. His few romantic entanglements had showed him a little more of himself and taught him something about the world at the same time. He remembered each coupling by the lesson, and by the way he'd felt slightly or completely different when their energies intertwined. Neither altogether good nor altogether bad, his most recent string of memories were of a woman he'd been both sad and relieved to see go. Link found it a little disappointing that one of the greatest lessons he had learned from her was that nice sheets actually mattered.

He had been even more disappointed when the nice sheets he bought somehow disappeared when she did; it wasn't until Link took up sleeping as a pastime that he purchased a new set. They might not get changed as often as before, but they were a sure step up from the thin scratchy coverings that he had spread across the sleeping surface in the interim.

Despite the pill kicking in, and those inner eyelids popping suddenly open, Link kept his actual eyes closed. A landscape swirled into perfect existence before him, and in the same moment his limbs became very heavy. Link had no doubt that he could lift his arms if he wanted to; but why would he want to? Dreams had always been a vivid and wakeful thing for him, but this was different.

Link was staring at a display screen, with characters stretched in digital overlay across a very realistic picture of space. It even seemed that he was moving, getting closer to some stars and further away from others. The lack of control in his body seemed to extend to the dream, and Link could not turn to look over his shoulder at whatever was behind him. For several minutes he stared at the lifelike image, stretching from wall to wall and floor to ceiling before him. It took up his entire visual field, the characters beautiful incomprehensibility while forever stretched out in starry spaciousness beyond them.

A sound came from behind him, a steady stream of what would have been words had he understood them. It was like no language he had ever heard, spoken in a smooth melodic tone. The desire to turn his back on the spacious image grew within him, and Link wondered again what was behind him. The voice continued speaking, and he kept staring through the illusion of glass to the eternal nothingness beyond.

It was strange to feel himself inside this dream, inside this experience. Even his body felt different, and Link felt his attention turning inward. As he watched space flowing forever past at what seemed a both interminably slow pace and somehow blindingly fast at the same time, he let his awareness move to his own breathing.

Except that it wasn't his own breathing.

Had he been in control of the process, Link surely would have paused his breath as he realized it. It went on instead, steady and smooth and with a depth to it that sent a spiraling thrill up his spine with each inhale. As a student of sleep, these last few months, he had also become a student of breath. All of the relaxing and invigorating exercises he had found were different than this. Link had seen results from playing around with various breathing techniques, but this was a whole new world for him.

For some reason, Link thought to follow the breath. It was all he could do, other than stare at the overwhelming view of what he could only describe as deep space. He would never tell anyone that his sleeping self often wondered if he was being taught something, either by his deeper consciousness or some other-worldly one; he had no one to tell, and it surely wouldn't make sense outside the confines of his own awareness within the dream state.

Following the breath was not nearly as simple as letting

his mind be blown by the vivid imagery of its own creation. It was all too easy to wonder how accurate his unconscious map of the stars might be, and where his drowsing brain might have placed him among them. Still he concentrated, and tried to sync his thought of breathing with the strange but somehow comfortable pattern.

Link had only meant to track it in his mind, to watch the pattern and try to imitate it later. When he felt a distant rising and falling, and felt that it was his own body breathing, Link suddenly felt his awareness volleying back and forth between the vivid scene and his own soft sheets. In mere moments, he had bounced back and forth a dozen times; Link reeled in the dizzying silent aftermath, and heard words reach his ears through the confusion.

"It would at least behoove you to acknowledge me," the words said, in a strangely tinny masculine tone. "There was a time when our views were of equal importance, even in your eyes."

In the same moment that Link realized he was still in the otherworldly setting, he realized that the body he was inhabiting was turning around. There was another fleeting sensation of his own body, lying somewhere far away, and the slippery sense that now would be a good time to open his eyes.

Link drifted in the dream, watching the view change as the eyes he was looking through turned to the voice he could suddenly understand. Another voice erupted, more masculine and less tinny; and Link heard it from within, like he was accustomed to hearing his own.

"That was before you betrayed me," it said. "That was before you tried to take control of my fleet."

"Admiral." The tinny voice came again, as Link got a look at what was speaking. "You are not in charge or in possession of this fleet. There is—"

It looked almost completely human, other than the dull metallic covering that served as its skin. All one color, the metal appeared soft and pliable; only that and its eyes gave it away as something less than natural. Its eyes were shaped like a person's, but were illuminated by the soft blue glow of active electricity. The way it moved was smooth and deliberate, while its face was expressing emotion and depth as clearly as its voice had been. Link found himself marveling at the creature, even as he reminded himself that it was only a dream.

In a flash, the body he was inhabiting moved. One arm stayed at his side, while the other snatched a sidearm from his hip. A silent burst of purple lightning erupted from the barrel, too fast to see and too bright to miss; and the creature exploded into a dozen pieces. Shards of metal and glass littered the floor as it collapsed, and bare sparking wires danced in the burst remains. The lump smoked and sputtered for a moment after it fell, to finally lie silent and fully extinguished.

Link felt his eyes go wide in wonder, and he smiled.

"Wow," he said, aloud.

The body he was in took a step back, surprised at the exclamation. Link swirled in his own confused bewilderment; the sound that had escaped those lips had not been the word he had uttered, but he had understood it as if it had the same meaning. It was all too much for him; the next time he became aware of soft sheets, Link dove at that awareness with all he had.

The last glimpse he had was of a half-dozen tiny trundling machines, appearing from hidden panels to converge on the pieces of robot that lay on the floor.

THREE

Sweat had moistened the sheets to the point of causing him discomfort, and it was suddenly easier to get out of bed than it had been in some time. His own body seemed awkward and unwieldy, his breathing jagged and shallow. Link put the dream from his mind as best he could, standing beside his bed and staring blankly at the clock on his nightstand.

The strange scene had played out in moments, a few minutes at most. It was nearly noon, according to the digital display. Link let befuddlement cloud his thoughts, felt his face scrunch with it as he watched the minute tick one digit closer to twelve o'clock. A dull ache had started in his head while he slept, and it took him another full minute to do the morning math.

"Caffeine," Link muttered under his breath. "Must have caffeine."

He laughed aloud, at his own struggled sentence. Link thought of the comic book heroes he had loved as a kid, and how they would state their intentions at a time when it seemed they should be focusing on the task at hand. When a building began falling or someone needed to be saved, a thought or speech bubble always seemed to accompany the action that stretched the limits of their super abilities.

"Got to...hold up...this building," or, "got to...save the...girl" sounded way more impressive than his mantra, but Link had to power through both the task at hand and the lack of super powers. His struggle seemed both genuine and comical to him, at the same time.

"Must...have...caffeine," he repeated, turning on the machine and watching it warm up with great intensity. Although he drank a lot of coffee, it was seldom all at once; Link had purchased a coffee maker that would make him a fresh cup every time, the way he consumed it. When it notified him that it was ready to brew, he selected a roast and slid the little plastic cup filled with grounds into place.

"Must...have...caffeine," he muttered again, closing the lid on the device and pressing a button. He stared at it while it brewed, watching the stream of darkened liquid shoot into the cup until it had stopped completely. To further entertain himself, he shuffled like a zombie to the refrigerator and pulled it slowly open.

"Must...have...caffeine," he said to the creamer, as he pulled it from the cold. He said it again as he was pouring, and once more while he stirred. Link's mantra had gone from superhero self-talk to undead moan in a half dozen repetitions, and he smiled while he sipped at last.

Almost immediately, the headache began to go away. His eyes widened, his thoughts cleared, and Link let the smile fall from his face.

Carrying the cup into the bedroom, he stood over the bed and looked down at it almost disdainfully. He sipped the warm brew while he went over the dream in his mind, and was nearly halfway done drinking it when he set it on the nightstand.

Stripping the sheets and replacing them with fresh ones was done in that same distracted state of mind, and he didn't stop to think of why he would do it now until it was done. Link's eyes went from the remaining coffee to the freshly made bed three or four times before he realized that he was making a decision. Doffing his pajamas, he slipped between the sheets and rested his head on a clean and crisp pillowcase.

Link sighed deeply, and let his eyes drift closed. Darkness greeted him, but he opened his eyes before it could entangle him deeply. That coffee was getting cold, and the pills were right there; it seemed only obvious that he should take one with the other, and either wake up completely or drift off entirely.

Sitting up in bed, he twisted the cap off the bottle and palmed one of the tiny mind-benders. It sat on his tongue until the coffee washed it away, down his throat to join the remains of the other in his belly. Link lay back and closed his eyes once more, waiting for the wakefulness.

While he waited, Link thought of the way he had been breathing in his dream. He felt the darkness seeping in, felt the warm sleepy tendrils burrow into his brain, and tried to imitate the pattern. It felt difficult and natural at the same time somehow, and it was a few minutes before he noticed a shift in his consciousness.

Darkness reigned, still; yet the thoughts echoing in that darkness were not his own. Link knew the patterns of his own mind, had watched them play out in that darkness as they shifted slowly over the years. In those last moments before he fell asleep, an urgency to do all the things he had been too timid to do that day would habitually fill his mind. It was no use to remind himself that it was too late, that the opportunities had existed in the moment and had passed; the only way to dupe his mind into sleeping would be to promise it that he would seize every opportunity tomorrow.

The next morning, he always woke to a different mind. Memories he hadn't thought of since childhood would surface, a sadness that he couldn't define would settle in, and it was all he could do to get himself out of bed in the morning. Somewhere in his sleep he had always lost the confidence that he mustered up the night before, and it was all he could do to make it through even the least demanding parts of his day.

This darkness was different. It was full of fury, and fire. It spoke to him of injustice, but not in a way that beat him down to nothing; Link felt an anger burning within him like he had never known, and the need to rise up and use it to change the world.

Link opened his eyes, sat up swiftly.

The room was dark, but there was no mistaking it for his own. Several dull green lights were visible, scattered throughout the inky blackness. A low steady thrumming sound filled his ears, and his body seemed to vibrate with it; he found it soothing rather than distracting, and had to listen closely to actually hear it. As he tried to listen, one of the green lights went blue. It began to move closer, and a voice sounded when it came near.

"Admiral," it said. "You are in a designated sleep period. You are advised to lie back, and close your eyes. Interrupting the sleep cycle is not conducive to optimal waking performance."

Narrowing his eyes in the darkness, Link could make out the form vaguely in the light it cast on itself. It was a twin to the machine he had seen earlier, distinctly human and robotic at the same time. Its voice was different than before, monotonous and mechanical.

Link laughed, moved his arms around like a puppet whose strings had been severed. The motions were useless and powerful at the same time, and he saw that his bare arms were thick with muscle. He peered at the light, raised an eyebrow in its direction.

"Admiral?" Link laughed again. "Did you call me Admiral?"

There was no response at first. Link continued leaning forward slightly, and felt his eyes go wide as the blue light shifted to green once more. When the response came, the voice was different and familiar all at once. There was texture and emotion to it, despite it having a distinctly tinny quality. It was the voice that had been speaking to him before, in the other dream.

"Is it you?" it said. "Have I found The Link?"

Link felt his eyes go even wider, at the sound of his name.

"Yes," he breathed. "I am Link."

It sounded strange, after he said it; so he amended the statement.

"I mean, my name is Link," he said, awkwardly. "I'm probably not the only one, though I don't think it's the most common name. Actually, it's a nickname. My real name is—"

"You have to help me," the voice said, cutting him off. "The man whose body you are inhabiting is preparing to kill half of the fleet. After one horrific decimation, he is determined to follow through with yet another. The first cost us our planet, and I fear that the next could lead to our extinction. You have to help me."

Link watched the light, willing his eyes to adjust as the speaker went on. When he didn't respond immediately, the voice came again.

"You have to help me," it insisted, once more.

Link laughed, leaned back, and closed his eyes.

"What a weird dream," he muttered, as the darkness took him.

FOUR

Now that he knew what kind of effect the pills had on his dreams, Link saw no reason to waste them on his waking hours. The drudgery of cubicle life was best served through a dim fog, in his experience; the aftermath of sleeping through the chemically induced sensory overload cast that dim fog like nothing else. His challenge was not in completing his work load; it was in making that work load last an entire eight hours. Sometimes he made mistakes, deliberately, so he could correct them later; it gave him something to do, with some of that time. He didn't like standing around the water cooler and talking about television, like his co-workers; so he surfed the internet between tasks, and looked for opportunities to meet people he might connect with.

It was not just unusual for someone to pop their head into his space, as much as they did it to each other; it was hard for him to remember it ever happening before.

"Hey," said the head, when it popped in.

A pretty face was attached to it, tanned with a smattering of freckles about a slightly upturned nose and across her high cheeks. Her eyes were like her hair, dark in color while reflecting every nearby light at every angle. She seemed to pick up the light and carry it with her, while radiating it outward at the same time. A body followed the face into his cubicle, and the space was suddenly filled with her scent and presence.

"Is it Lincoln?" she asked, smiling. "Is that right?"

The smile lit up the tiny enclosed area, and Link found it too bright in his cubicle to string together the words to tell her that the friends he didn't have called him Link.

Dumbly, he nodded.

"I'm Sherry," she said.

Link nodded again. He knew that. He also knew it would be a bit creepy to say so, and there were still no clever groupings of words leaping to mind; so he remained silent.

"There's a Christmas party on Saturday," she said, holding something out to him. "Are you going to be able to make it?"

There was a word, somewhere in the blinding brilliance. Link grabbed at it, vocalized it as triumphantly as possible.

"Uh..."

She watched him reach further, and must have seen him fail. Leaning forward, Sherry put the thing she had been holding on his desk. She flashed him with one last smile, and left him to breathe in whatever part of her lingered after she left. After several stunned minutes Link reached out, and picked up the printed flyer.

'DID YOU KNOW THAT OVER SEVENTY PERCENT OF YOUR CO-WORKERS DON'T HAVE FAMILY NEARBY?'

The first line jumped out at him, and Link shrugged in answer.

"So?" he muttered. "Who needs family?"

The flyer went on, in all caps.

'IN A RECENT OFFICE POLL, MANY OF YOU RESPONDED THAT YOU WOULD BE ALONE FOR

THE HOLIDAYS. SEVERAL PEOPLE SAID THEY WOULD BE AVAILABLE TO WORK, AT NORMAL SALARY, EVEN THOUGH THEY ARE BEING GIVEN PAID TIME OFF.'

There was a line of sideways frowning faces, made from punctuation marks. Under that was another batch of text, still boldly capitalized.

'MANAGEMENT WOULD LIKE TO SHOW OUR APPRECIATION FOR YOUR HARD WORK AND DEDICATION THROUGHOUT THE YEAR. THAT'S WHY WE ARE THROWING A CHRISTMAS EVE OFFICE PARTY!'

The day and time were in smaller print, at the bottom of the page. Under that, it offered two ways to RSVP: Link felt his eyes go wide as he read the last line.

It was Sherry's e-mail address and mobile phone number.

Rather than think back over all the times he had promised himself that he would ask for that information in the past, Link simply wasted no time in adding the number to his meager list of contacts. He even started to type out a couple of texts to her without any intention of finishing or sending them.

After awhile, he went back to work. His paced his duties so he would be neither the fastest nor the slowest person entering similar data, so he might continue his lifelong deliberate practice of living somewhere in the middle. Link hated to call it mediocrity, since so many people seemed to hover right around where he did; instead he thought of it as home.

Again, best seen through the forgiving filter of a dim fog.

Looking at the flyer was pointless, and a little annoying; although neither thought kept him from glancing at it between batches of work. Each time his eyes landed on it, Link grew slightly more irritated. He hated it when people used all capital letters to express themselves, and the only thing he hated more than emoticons were imitation emoticons made from punctuation marks.

Still, Sherry had been on his radar since her first day. She had started below him, only to work her way into his position and then past it. Now she was lower management, which had put her more out of reach than ever. Saying hello to her had gone from a simple cubicle pop-in to an office visit in a day, and Link remained convinced that it had been the day he was finally going to pop in.

He found himself staring at the flyer again, thinking maybe people who used capital letters too much were not so bad after all. Then it was as though someone else had control of his hands, and suddenly Link was typing another message to her number.

'Hi Sherry,' it said. 'I'll see you at the party.'

Link pressed send, his heart pounding in his chest. A moment later he smacked his forehead with the flat of one hand, and typed another message.

'This is Lincoln, BTW.'

When he pressed the icon to ship off the message, a little bubble popped up to show him that she was preparing to respond.

Link felt his heart beating even faster.

'Great, Lincoln!' popped up, finally. 'See you there!'

Without thinking, he shot off another message.

'My friends call me Link.'

He felt like a complete idiot the moment he sent it, and locked his phone to blank the screen and stew in his stupidity.

The phone buzzed on his desk.

Link snatched it up, and pressed the home button.

'Link it is,' she had written. 'See you at the party!'

He nearly hopped to his feet and whooped. Instead Link silently opened his phone, sighed with relief, and edged a little further out on the limb he was on.

'Save me a dance?'

Before he could reconsider, he stabbed at the phone and sent the message. A slow steady flush crept up the back of his neck; by the time the phone buzzed again, Link felt like his skull was on fire.

'I don't think it's that kind of party.'

Link frowned, reading it, and felt the burn. Of course it wasn't that kind of party. What was this, high school? He read the message over and over, shaking his head at his own bumbling.

Another message popped up while he read it over, below the first, and his eyebrows shot up.

'We'll see.'

A wide grin spread across his face, and Link had to bite his forearm to keep from letting out that whoop from earlier when the phone buzzed one last time.

'You're cute.'

Spending the rest of the day correcting his own absent-minded and now unintentional mistakes was worth it. Instead of annoying Link, it amused him. He still finished everything he needed to get done before it was time to go home, like he always did. There were messages on his phone to read over and over again, and that seemed to pass the time like nothing else.

When the clock released him at last, Link found he was not looking forward to going home and spending the evening with Sherry's messages. His thoughts shifted as soon as he got in his car, and Link found himself looking forward to nice sheets and another experiment in sleeping with the wakeful drug.

FIVE

On the one hand, there was the fear of not taking enough. The real moment of clarity and control had begun with him taking two pills, and Link had no interest in playing an observer's role when he could play an active one. Whatever this dream was going to present, as far as options, he wanted to be the one choosing his own adventure.

On the other hand, he only had the one prescription. It had not been marked for automatic refill, and he hadn't even checked until after he had taken the two so close together. Three months' worth of pills would only last six weeks at that rate, unless he figured out some way to get more.

In the end, he laughed himself into a compromise. He had no evidence that the dream would even be the same when he went back to sleep, or that the effects of the drug would not change quickly as his unique body chemistry adjusted to the shift. Sunday had been a dreamless respite, after all; perhaps that's how his sleep would go, from here on out.

He'd take two pills, and fall asleep. When he woke up, he would know how to proceed.

Link laughed at himself again, for being so excited about what awaited him on the other side of unconsciousness. Just today, he had gotten a touch closer to someone he had been admiring from afar for as long as he could remember.

If it had been yesterday, he wouldn't have been able to sleep for thinking about the deeper meaning of the brief and meaningless exchanges they'd had. Now, he was afraid he wouldn't nod off for all the excitement he was having about a dream he could only visit by sleeping.

As he took the pills, Link wondered for a brief moment if one explained the other, and that he perhaps deserved to be alone if all it took was a fantastical story manufactured by his unconscious mind to get him to unplug from what little life he had.

Getting ready for bed, the thought washed away like so much toothpaste foam. Everyone's got reasons they don't deserve anyone, and everyone's got reasons why they do; some folks, they just get lucky.

The lonely little bed was comfortable, and his excitement was not such that he could not sleep. Almost immediately after shutting his eyes, Link began to see lights in the darkness. His first thought was that they were of an altogether different hue from any of the lights he had seen on Earth. As he felt himself moving towards them, his thoughts seemed to drift alongside him in some kind of visible form. Link thrilled at the gossamer strands of drifting nothingness, and then they were gone.

His next thought, somehow, was not his own.

"Only a fool," he muttered, "would not take defensive action."

Link found himself staring at a log book. He knew it was a log book because it had 'Admiral's Log' printed across the top in bold letters. Otherwise, it was an object that was simultaneously familiar and foreign. Slim and pliable, it was really a sheet of metal stretched over a desktop. It felt padded, thin as it was, and gave way under his touch to make incoherent marks on the surface. The marks appeared under the words that had already been written, in neat printed form, likely using the pointed device he was holding over the sheet in the other hand that wasn't his. It could only be described as a stylus, and had a glowing blue dot halfway down the slim barrel. Link touched it to the surface, and another meaningless mark appeared. He set it down, and the light went off immediately.

The log was not much thicker than a piece of construction paper, and Link couldn't resist toying with the edges. They came up easily, and he was able to roll the sheet into a metal scroll of sorts. He unrolled it, smoothed it out flat, and tried folding it over. Biting his lip as a crease formed on the fold, he smoothed it out quickly once more. No new line or bend or flaw of any kind marked the screen, and the words that had been written there were still in the same perfect neat form. Link shrugged, and folded it over on itself again. He kept folding it in half, until it was a neat rectangle of metal he could slip into his pocket like a folded sheet of paper. Unfolding it, he was able to smooth the surface out into its original flat shape; his palm didn't leave marks, but a single finger would.

All of the random smears from his efforts were slight, or under the words that had been written in the log. The words were naturally in a language that he couldn't read, until he tried to read them. When he made that effort, he found that the words now didn't make sense from a contextual standpoint. They were all brief entries, made in a kind of shorthand that left out many of the words that they would have needed to form full coherent thoughts.

-Engineering detected new gravity pull; investigating.
-Fleet differences growing more pronounced; dangerous.
-Mining operation damages; assess risk.
-Magnetic fields affecting memory; potential opportunity?

-Platinum Star team leader losing ground; make an example.

-Silver Star team leader showing

The last entry ended midway through, and made as little sense to him as the rest of them had.

He wasn't sure what chilled him more: reading the entries or watching the flashing images behind his eyes as he did. Link was completely himself, somehow, in an entirely different body. He felt a tension in him, at his center, where he usually felt a dull distant ache. It was a strange thing to make note of, since he had never even made note of the pain before. Now it was gone, and simultaneously replaced with a fire that felt like it would burn him if he did not somehow stay out in front of it.

Pushing himself away from the desk, Link stood and looked for a reflective surface. He watched his own mind, as he moved, racing through useless thoughts like it was so accustomed to doing. Reading in dreams is not possible, even if the language it's written in is one you grew up reading; that's what the dream experts say, anyway. Also, the way thoughts come to you is totally different; he knew that from his own experience. No matter how lucid his dreams might have been or seemed, nothing had plunked him so completely into another reality like this.

Even the pills came to mind, and how he would definitely be taking two at a time as long as he continued to get these mysterious results. It was followed by the clear thought that he should really not be thinking of such things so clearly. By the time Link found a mirror to inspect himself in, he'd had all kinds of thoughts that seemed an awful lot more like waking thoughts than sleeping thoughts to him.

None of them disturbed him as much as the reflection.

The face was his, only it wasn't. Much like the colors had

seemed slightly off, as he passed through whatever doorway his mind had thrust him through, so did his features. His eyes were still brown, but the dullness had been replaced by a stark shining luminosity. The lines on his face were smooth, the flesh full and tight, while somehow looking as though this face had weathered a good many more years than his own. He tried to smile, and immediately let it fall. Link's smile was awkward, and unnatural; this one was severe, and humorless. Resting, this face had a fierce expression that Link had never seen shape his own features; his resting face looked sad, from what people and pictures told him.

The only things he had noticed in the room were the items that seemed familiar in some way: the journal, the bunk, the books, and the mirror he had found at last. A sound came from somewhere in the room while he was inspecting the similar features, and he turned toward it involuntarily.

It wasn't a beep or a ring, the way a beep or a ring might sound; nonetheless, it had some quality of an urgent tone to it, and he wondered what it might be.

"Hello?" Link said. "Is someone there?"

His voice sounded strange to him, in much the same way everything else did. Instead of being completely different than his own, or exactly the same, it landed somewhere in between that he wasn't sure he liked.

"May I enter?"

The other voice was coming from the same wall as the sound had come from, and Link moved another step closer to it. He looked around, seeing the scattering of unfamiliar objects as if for the first time. He shook his head.

"Uh, sorry," he said. "It's not a good time."

Link sighed, assuming it would not be transmitted along with his message. It was comforting to know that he had control of the room, and that he could explore it at his leisure without interruption. He moved to the first unfamiliar object, reaching out tentative hands that looked so much like his own in the direction of the strange item.

Another sound came behind him, and Link spun in place to see a part of the wall disappear. Nothing slid aside, or opened up; and as far as he could tell whatever created the opening had not caused the sound. That was coming from the other side of the opening, a collection of new noises as unfamiliar as the object Link had been about to grab. There was a figure framed by the sudden opening, and the strange din filled the space behind it; the figure was completely silent, standing there, until it spoke.

"The Link?" it said. "Is that you?"

He felt his own strangely familiar eyes go wide, at the sound of his name. The thing he was looking at was not the same thing he had spoken to before. It was a bit too much for him to process in the moment, and Link stood there staring wide-eyed at the collection of gears and mechanisms a moment longer than it had patience for.

"Of course," it said. "It is you."

It made noise now, other than talking in that tinny inhuman tone that this particular speaker had taken on. Gears moved, and it trundled into the room with a distinctly strange hum. The wall formed again behind it, and it began speaking once more as soon as it did.

"I knew it was you," it said, "when I saw you toying with the log and looking at yourself at length in the mirror. The Admiral wouldn't do those things, like that. It had to be you. Don't worry, I was able to remotely erase the marks you made. Your presence must remain undetected."

Link had never imagined that he would be describing the sound of a robot's voice to himself, in his head; he certainly never thought he would have called it gleeful.

This collection of what could only be called metal definitely sounded gleeful, even if it was a tinny-sounding glee. He frowned, darkly, as an angry thought grabbed at his mind.

"You were watching me?" he demanded. "In private?"

He wasn't sure what it was using for eyes, or if it saw him in the traditional sense at all. The feeling that the thing was looking at him could have been completely in his head, from what he knew of the odd mechanisms at work in the smooth reflective surfaces.

"Private?"

It repeated the word, as if it were an unfamiliar one. The next sound that issued forth could only be described as laughter. Being tinny, like nearly every other sound the thing was making, the laugh put Link off more than a little bit.

"A primitive and ancient concept," it said. "In our society."

Link felt his hand began to shake, and spoke the first words that came to mind.

"I want to destroy you," he said. "I know I can, and I feel like I want to. I have to admit, I don't know if I can resist the urge."

It felt good, to threaten the thing, although he didn't know why.

Rather than wheel away, the collection of alien mechanisms moved closer.

"That is the thought pattern of the body you are inhabiting," it said. "You can resist that, and you can learn to take complete control of both the thoughts and actions of the body. That is what you are here for. It is what your mind tells me would be called a destiny, by your people. This is your destiny, to stop the man you appear to be from doing many others great harm."

Link stared at the thing, trying not to laugh. This was a little heavy for him, even if it was a dream.

"I'm sorry, little robot," he smiled. "I don't think I'm the guy you're looking for. From my perspective, this whole world is just a dream. Dreams are for fun, not for being bossed around by contraptions that talk about silly things like destiny."

Something started whirring in some part of the metallic housing, and the thing shuddered while remaining in place.

"Does this feel like a dream?" it demanded.

Link laughed, and looked around. He couldn't name more than half of the things he saw, or pair them with a purpose in his mind; the only thing that seemed more unlikely than his surroundings was whatever he was having a conversation with, which seemed to be doing everything it could to get on his nerves.

The anger didn't feel natural, to his way of thinking; but the body he was in had acutely tuned into it. Link relaxed his hold on it, and surprised himself utterly when he did.

His hand leapt to his side, unbidden. It snatched a small weapon of some kind from the belt at his waist, aimed and fired in less than a startled breath. In the same automatic motion, he holstered the sidearm. The waist-high collection of moving parts exploded into a dozen pieces in front of him, and Link moved abruptly to sit at the seat he had vacated earlier in his search for a mirror. He watched the hand he was no longer in control of complete the last sentence he had glanced at in the log.

-Silver Star team leader showing promise; test her.

After the words had been written, Link read them. He had a brief moment where he felt as though he was getting smaller, somehow; then he disappeared, and tumbled into a different kind of darkness.

SIX

Before the pills, Link had considered himself an expert on tuning out and getting through. The knowledge of any impending situation was enough to start the anxious twist in his belly, and he tolerated it when it came by embracing the anxiety. He was well practiced at shutting off the connection between his brain and his face, and had the habit of wearing a slight frown when his own features wanted to twist along with his emotional center.

Now, it was different.

A thin veneer of dream haze was painted over his entire experience now, and Link was able to tune out and get through like never before. Becoming aware of the knot of tension within him had made him both a casual observer to his own pain and a fully engaged participant in it. Watching it tighten within him was a full-time job, and he found that he had little attention to put towards anything else.

He knew he was at work, and that the tasks he needed to complete were on track to be finished when the clock was. Otherwise, he could not have been more dimly aware of the moments that passed or what events they trundled past his senses. The office buzzed with the usual sounds, phones ringing and people chatting idly. Link tuned it all out, drifting through the day in a pleasantly detached cloud.

Most of the day was spent at his desk, building columns in a digital universe or surfing the internet to kill all the hours in the day he didn't need. At lunch, he slid his cooler from under his desk and ate the fare he had brought from home. The only place Link needed to go where he couldn't avoid people was the restroom, and that's where he found himself engaged by one.

"Hey."

Link was standing in front of the urinal, doing his business and paying very little mind to much else. His skull felt like an empty chamber, with cotton clinging to every surface like soft stalactites and stalagmites. The dullness was like a sound, and the sound itself was dull; for a long moment of quiet calm, he thought a voice in his head had escaped through his mouth.

He realized, suddenly, that it had been someone else entirely.

Turning his head was not an option, no matter the state of his sluggish mind. Link continued to keep his eye on the task in hand, and frowned. He wanted to say that this was not the place for conversation, or for any kind of interaction whatsoever. A part of him wanted to voice his thoughts on shared restrooms, and how he thought it was a strange concept to begin with; but, after all, this was not the place for voicing thoughts.

"Hey," he echoed, instead.

There was not a full second between his single word ending and the other man's next sentence beginning. Like a wire tripping a mine, the sound set off a long rattle of a response. Link finished before he was done, zipping up and flushing. He walked past the man, frowning as fiercely as he could, and stopped at the sink.

"I'm Steve," the guy said. "I just started this week. I

haven't seen you around. Are you one of the cubicle rats? I am. Are you in sales or data entry? I'm totally happy with the data entry job, so far, They don't expect much, but I plan on really wowing upper management. And middle management. Especially that one, Sherry I think is her name. You know who I'm talking about? Of course you do. She's single, right?"

Link caught his own eye in the mirror, while washing his hands. He exchanged a look with his reflection, as if to say 'can you believe this guy' without saying anything at all. Steve zipped up and moved between Link and the paper towel dispenser, and stuck out his hand.

"What's your name?" he said.

His eyes darted to the man's hand, outstretched and waiting. Link looked at his own, still dripping from the washing. A whole string of appropriate things came into his mind, that he might say to Steve: this was not a place to make friends, or even to talk to friends you had already made; or that there was no way on Earth he was ever shaking that hand, under any circumstances.

Link didn't say any of them; he opted for a single word, instead.

"Ugh."

Link wiped his hands on his slacks, stepped past him and pushed the door open with his shoulder. As it sighed shut behind him, he said it aloud once more.

"Ugh."

He was paying as little attention to his surroundings as he had been all day, and Link didn't realize that he was not alone in the hallway.

"What was that?"

Link turned at the voice, his hand poised to wave away the comment. When he saw who it was, he kept turning. His wave of dismissal turned to a friendly little wave of greeting, and he felt as much like an ass as he must have looked while putting on his most realistic smile.

"Hey, pretty girl," he said. "That was nothing. Sorry, just being completely honest with myself about how I feel about someone else."

He spread his hands.

"Not you, of course," he added. "I'm somewhat fond of you."

His heart had started pounding the moment he saw her, and his reaction to seeing her surprised him even more.

Did I just call her 'pretty girl'? Link thought, flushing. *Did I just say that I'm 'somewhat fond of her'? What is this, the fifties? Europe?*

She giggled, and his tension eased a little. A smile brightened her features, and Link felt as though his own was beginning to go more than skin deep. At that moment, the door opened and Steve entered the hallway. Link let his smile fall immediately, and rolled his eyes.

"Hey!"

Steve was as exuberant as he had been in the washroom, smiling at them in turn. He pointed at Link's pants, where he had wiped his hands, and smirked.

"Uh-oh," he said. "Looks like you got a little on you."

The flush had already crept up the back of his neck, to set his scalp aflame. Link felt the blood rush to his face as he sneered back.

"You were standing between me and the paper towels," he said. "I had to choose between wiping my hands on my pants and shaking hands with an animal that doesn't have the decency to wash or keep quiet in the bathroom."

He looked down, at the stains.

"I chose well," he added. "In case you're too daft to get that too."

What should have been the most awkward moment of his work day had somehow become his most triumphant moment in recent memory. All he had to do was stare at the guy, at this point, and hope he would slink away. Link made sure that Sherry didn't see his sigh of relief, when Steve actually decided to move off without saying more. She looked at him, not knowing that this was not the guy Link knew himself to be.

"Really?" she said, glancing after him. "Did he really not wash his hands? That's so gross."

Link had to make sure his eyes didn't gleam, with the blood pumping through his veins or with his delight at her comment.

"Right?" he said. "Hygiene is so important."

He was puffing his chest out a little, without knowing that he had done it. His shoulders even felt more broad, until he thought back over his words. They dropped, then; and his chest deflated. The statement had not been nearly as testosterone-driven as his verbal attack on Steve.

"So, uh..." Link began.

The shroud of fog was back, and his thoughts went somewhere completely different than where he was at the moment. Link shuffled his feet, and watched them like they belonged to someone else. Every time he glanced up at Sherry, it looked like she was about to say something or was hoping that he would; so, he stopped glancing up at her. Something in their dynamic had changed, and Link couldn't put his finger on what it was.

"Back to work, then," he mumbled, feebly.

As he pivoted in place, and felt the flush climbing his back once more, she said his name. Hearing it from her lips was like a cool stream of fresh water, quenching the fire of his embarrassment.

"Link," she said. "My name is Sherry."

He stopped, and hesitated to turn. His face still felt flush, even if his heart pounded now for a different reason altogether. Before he could respond, she spoke again.

"But I like 'pretty girl', too," she added.

Link stood there, his back turned and his mind whirling. In the absence of anything clever or even fully formulated leaping promptly to mind, he chose to walk away smiling.

SEVEN

All of his internet searches, both at home and at work, were about the drug he was taking. Link learned that some notoriously smart people were using it to be smart for more hours in a day, but there was nearly nothing on how it affected people who took it right before going to sleep. Most reports on the dreams that others had experienced on the drug were footnotes in studies focused on other results; he found more anecdotal comments than anything, and slogging through all of them was slow going.

Nightmares were neither common nor uncommon, according to the studies, and lucid dreams seemed to be featured heavily in any mention of positive effects the pills had on sleep time and quality. No one said that they went to another world, or visited the same spaceship every night when they went to bed. Even if they had, he realized after searching for them exhaustively, what would he do about it? Send them an email, try to have lunch with them in another galaxy sometime?

Nothing made any sense, except pursuing the one thing in his life that he felt genuinely curious about. His own errant behavior had already made him lose interest in Sherry a bit, as he couldn't stop wondering if she would expect the brazen attitude he had displayed earlier to show up every time Link did. Whoever he was, Link was not that guy. Thinking back over his interactions with both her and Steve, all he wanted to do was take a shower and go to sleep.

The anger that lingered was of no interest to Link. He had no desire to examine why he had stepped from his comfort zone for a moment, why he resented Sherry for liking it, or why he loathed his own stew of thoughts. Hopefully the shower would wash away the whole mess, and the sleep would make him completely forget about all of it. At least in his dreams, he didn't have to wonder about the strange story unfolding behind his eyes; it was just a dream, after all.

Link could only remind himself of that so many times in a day, before he started analyzing why he was repeating it like a mantra to his muddled mind. He reminded himself of it again when he noticed that he could see a visible difference in how full the bottle of pills was. After careful consideration, and another broken record reminder, he decided to take only one of them.

Lying down, he closed his eyes and watched his breaths. They looked different than before, and he began to marvel at how he might have taken on a complicated new breathing pattern while living through one of the most unconscious weeks of his life. The doorway came at him like before, and he slipped through it easily as his thoughts drifted from his mind with no effort on his part. Link looked out through open eyes, without opening his own.

Two people were strapped to chairs, directly before him. They both looked agitated, but in completely different ways. The woman was frowning fiercely, her face and eyes set in a look of determination that made her look striking in a way the most complicated features never could. Her eyes were dark, but they glowed with a pain and a promise that Link could only guess at.

The man was in pain, as well. He was not bearing up under it like the woman, and his face seemed twisted by fear more than it was set in any kind of stubborn defiance to it. Link found his eyes going back to the woman, although it was not his will that made them move.

No one paid attention to the other figure in the featureless space; he sat in the shadows, turning dials and punching buttons on a small device in his lap.

"You have barely served a quarter cycle," Link said.

It wasn't him saying it, except that his lips moved and his voice issued forth. Wherever the thoughts that propelled the words were coming from, it wasn't his decision when they came out. In all honesty, none of it even made real sense to him. As he watched, his voice went on.

"Your performance has been exemplary," he said. "You went from top flyer to team leader in less time than anyone ever has."

Link felt a smile stretch the corners of his lips, although there was nothing in their pain to smile about. A dark chuckle poured out of him, and he nodded against his will.

"Even me," he added, still smiling humorlessly.

The young woman's eyes narrowed almost imperceptibly, and her stubbornness showed in her own fixed expression. Link watched his field of vision shift as the body he was in did, and his gaze came to rest on the man. He felt the smile fall, and his own eyes narrow.

"You," he said. "You've never impressed me. You may have impressed everyone else, but not me. Everything you do is so rote, and practiced. There is no imagination in you, only a long list of rules that you unconsciously live by. I thought you excelled at mediocrity, and taking orders; and that was reason enough to let you lead, along with the way everyone responded to you. I thought you lacked the imagination to do anything but what you were told, and that was exactly what I was looking for in my top team leader."

Link leaned in, and heard his own voice go lower.

"You get the most promising and experienced flyers," he said.

He glanced at her.

"She gets the worst," he added.

His eyes settled on the man again.

"She gets more out of them than you," he said. "Which was fine, until today. Today she came to me, to do something terrible."

Link felt the form he was inhabiting straighten, and he walked along with it to tower over the other prisoner once more. Every cell in the other man's body felt like it was on fire, aching to let everyone around him feel the burn. He didn't know what kind of pain the two people strapped to the chair were experiencing, only that they were; beads of sweat stood out on both of their brows, and they were each trembling from head to toe. Link felt like he shared some electrical connection with them, and that he was feeding on their agony.

"Top flyer," he spat, glaring at her.

"Natural leader," he went on, "and brilliant strategist. And now this. You have branded yourself turncoat, and called out the top team leader on the most egregious of all crimes. Why would you do this?"

Out of the corner of his eye, Link saw the man drop his shoulders ever so slightly. A new fire burned within him, and somehow the rising anger only made his voice even more calm.

"You know the consequences," Link said.

The woman bore up under whatever was taxing her system, and looked him in the eye. The look was earnest, or challenging, or defiant; or all three. Link couldn't tell, until she spoke.

"I had to," she said. "For the sake of the fleet."

Her voice was trembling even more than her body was, and she took a deep practiced breath before speaking again. Link watched a bead of sweat run from her forehead to her chin, unnoticed and unchecked.

"He came to me," she said, "to inform me of the central system's plan to remove you from power."

She sighed painfully, heaved in a labored breath, and went on.

"You had to know," she gasped. "No matter the cost to me."

Link was squirming under the other man's skin. The pain evident in both of their faces and postures was disturbing to him, and it disturbed him even more to have to watch passively; but most disturbing was the joy he felt rising up in him. He felt alive, cracking with the energy that was being drained from the prisoners. Torn between watching the view through his eyes and the tide of explosive anger awash within him, Link rode along as the view moved to the man again.

"I won't ask," he said, "if this is true. I lose two leaders this day, either way. Even if every other aspect of your performances were exemplary, I cannot trust the accused or the accuser."

Part of him was unable to ignore the small details that the body he was in was watching for. Although his eyes were on the man, his attention was on the woman; he saw her posture stay resolute while the man's drooped even further. He spoke, bitterly, while she maintained her calm silence.

"You would be a tyrant," the man said. "You want blind allegiance, and you plan to kill everyone that does not give it. I had to try and stop you. For the good of the fleet."

The woman burst out laughing, despite her pain.

"There would be no fleet," she spat, "if he had not taken control. We would have burned with our brethren, and our people would be no more."

All eyes were on her, although Link still stood before the man. He saw her glance up at him, briefly, before dropping her chin to her chest to hide her next wave of pain. There was a reverence in her gaze that startled both him and the owner of the body he was in.

Link glanced at the man with the device, pointing at the one strapped to the chair.

"Give him all he can take," he said. "I'll be back in a few hours, to give him more."

His hand fell to his side, and his eyes went to her.

"End her pain," he said.

Link had a moment of terrified panic, and he thought he was about to see her go completely rigid and then go forever limp. Instead, her features relaxed and the trembling in her body stopped. She looked up at him, a puzzled expression on her face.

"I will figure out what to do with you later," he said.

He looked at the man with the device once more, and watched him turn the knobs in quiet delight for a few seconds.

"Get her to a cell," he said. "And bring me the code to open it. Only me."

EIGHT

After waking from the dream, Link found he was unable to get back to sleep. He was shaken, and felt like he might be sick. Instead, he rose before the sun did and began his morning ritual early. A shower and clean clothes made him feel a little better, and he took his second cup of coffee out on the cramped balcony that he seldom used. It was still dark, and he stared at the stars while he sipped at the steaming brew. Only the brightest could shine through the glow cast by the streetlights; Link fixated on one, then the next, until the nearest star began to light the sky.

Either he was a lot more twisted than he had ever thought, or he was visiting another world in his dreams. One seemed as likely as the other, but neither presented a clear or easy way out.

If he was working through his personal demons by personifying them in robots and people in his dreams, only to destroy or torture them, there was definitely something deeply wrong with him that the pills couldn't help with. On the other hand, if he was actually visiting another world... well, that put a whole different light on it.

Link shook his head, as the first rays of sunlight turned the brightest stars to pinpoints, and took his eyes off the distant fires. Instead he let them find a space between stars, dark and vacant but for the possibility of a spaceship inhabiting some of the emptiness between him and the rest of eternity.

Or a fleet of spaceships.

"They don't talk about their world," he muttered, under his breath. "They talk about their fleet."

Link drained the cooled remains of his coffee, and dug his phone from his pocket to check the time. He left behind the little balcony, likely for another several months, and took his thoughts with him to work. Between the pile of documents on his desk and the balancing act of deciding what he wanted to believe, the first couple of hours flew right by. The day was beginning to look like it would pass swiftly, and he would be all set to get to bed early. By the time a head poked into his cubicle, Link had made up his mind.

He would help the robot, and try to stop the body he kept jumping into from doing whatever it wanted to do. Looking at that man from the inside had terrified him, and watching him torture both ally and enemy had been enough to shake him to his core. Whatever that angry twisted mind was planning, it was clear that it wasn't good.

It was also clear that it wasn't Link's own mind that he was battling, from this perspective. If he failed, it only meant the death of some distant star stragglers that no one on Earth would ever know about; contemplating failure when it was his own well-being on the line was not an option, if he was to participate without the kind of anxiety gripping him that so often froze his thoughts and body alike.

The head that poked into his space was Steve's, and it had to say hello twice before Link registered hearing him. He swiveled his chair, slowly, to face the unwelcome intrusion head-on.

"Steve," he said.

He didn't ask what he could do for him, or what Steve was doing here. Link waited, wearing a look of practiced impatience, until the words came spewing forth.

Steve nodded.

"Lincoln," he said. "It's Lincoln, right? The boss says I need to work with you for a couple days, so you can train me on the software you guys use here. She said you really know what you're doing, and that you're the best person to show me the ropes."

He paused, and shifted uncomfortably.

"I know we got off on the wrong foot," Steve continued, "and I'm real sorry about all that. I shoot off my mouth, sometimes, especially when I'm nervous. I didn't know you and Sherry were a thing, and I didn't mean to be disrespectful. I'm nervous now too, if you can't tell. I hope I'm not saying something to further offend you, or put you off."

Link held up a hand, when he realized that this guy wasn't going to shut up unless he interrupted.

"Steve," he said. "Relax. Call me Link."

He didn't tell him that his friends called him that, so there would be no mistake made. An admission of anxiety went a lot way with him, though; and Link kind of liked the thought of helping him be a little less nervous. The way Steve was holding himself reminded him too much of the man he had seen strapped down and in agony not so long ago.

Rather than lower his hand, Link gestured with it.

"Go get a chair," he said, "and some way to take notes."

Steve nodded, exuberant, and started to turn away.

"Oh, and also," Link added. "Sherry and I are not a thing."

Steve reversed his movement, and cocked his head as he faced Link once more.

"Really?" he said. "You might want to tell her that.

I heard her talking about you, in the break room, and it sounded like you two were maybe definitely a thing."

Link felt his brow furrow, and he leaned forward in his chair. He wanted to ask what 'maybe definitely' meant, and what she had said exactly; for a long wondering moment, he wanted to ask all kinds of things. Remembering what Steve had said about running off at the mouth, and how doubtful he was that Sherry might respond to him in a positive fashion if he could ever manage to be himself around her, he waved his hand again.

"Go," he said. "Get your stuff. Let's have fun with coding."

With a sigh of relief and a friendly smile, Steve nodded and ducked back out of the cubicle. Before Link could congratulate himself on being extra nice to the guy, Steve was back and squeezing in next to him. The patter turned out to be more distracting than annoying, and by the end of the day Link was glad he had been chosen to do Steve's training.

NINE

Waking early had given him a calm that he wasn't accustomed to, and Link had actually found himself enjoying both work and Steve's company. The guy wasn't all bad, especially after he chilled out a little; and he learned quickly enough. They even had a few moments of laughter, and a couple of decent exchanges; but when Steve asked if he wanted to get a beer after work, Link had declined as politely as he could without letting on that he needed to get home so he could dream.

He took two pills within an hour of walking through the front door, and felt himself being pulled through that strange doorway almost right away. Link woke in the same place he had before, a dark room with random lights glowing softly to cast a dim luminescence over everything. This time a robot did not accost him when he moved; instead, a light began to get brighter, seeming to come from everywhere and nowhere all at once. The room came completely into lighted view, to show him all of the things he could not identify more clearly.

Link didn't want to do anything that might tip off the robot with electronic eyes everywhere, just yet. He wanted to explore, and see what more of the ship and the inside of this mind looked like. He moved toward the part of the wall that he had seen disappear, and it opened up as he neared. Suddenly, the dull rumbling sound that had become a soothing sonic backdrop was replaced by the din of rapid footfalls and strident voices raised in some kind of shared excitement.

Confidence was the most important part of any sham, and he put it on as best he could as he stepped out into the bustling hallway. People avoided eye contact with him, walking around his trajectory; and that made falling into a confident stride easier. Link walked at the same speed as the others, slipping from one flowing stream of striders to the next as he turned randomly up one hallway or another. They all seemed to be bustling with activity, and no one questioned his presence in any of them. At first he thought they were rushing to some emergency, the way they were moving just short of running. Then he saw some of the same faces again, and realized what was happening.

It was some shared exercise routine, and he had stepped out and into it without even knowing. He walked the halls even more confidently after he realized it, and even gave a couple of faces that he saw a third time a friendly nod. On every occasion, they nodded back and looked away immediately; each of them sped away after, and he never saw them again.

Once the hallways began to clear out, he tried to find the chamber he had left behind. It was no use, the way all the corridors looked the same. Link looked around for a quiet place, somewhere that he could behave strangely enough to draw the robot's attention. He found it in what looked like a giant but deserted dining room, with tables affixed to the floor in neat rows and swivel chairs attached at regular intervals along each side.

Link went to the nearest table, and sat down. He tried

waving his arms a little, after glancing around to make sure no one could see. Nothing happened, so he shrugged and spoke instead.

"Hey, robot," he said. "It's me, Link. Are you around?"

It was just like when the door opened in his chambers; a section of the wall nearby simply disappeared, and a square box trundled out. It rolled smoothly and soundlessly to the table he was sitting at, and stopped in front of him.

"I am not a robot," it said.

He couldn't tell where the voice was coming from, only that it sounded even more mechanical than it had through the other contraption.

Link shrugged.

"Sorry," he said. "You never told me your name."

The box looked as though it was there to clear dishes, and possibly wash them on the fly. Maybe it even stored them in its clunky frame, and set the table when it was time.

"I have no name," it said. "Even when I was alive, I had no name. I was known by my title, and it was one I could not have been more proud to bear. I was The Engineer, and I worked with the other leaders of our world to solve the problems of our planet and its people. There were nine of us, altogether—"

"So," Link cut him off, "I should call you 'The Engineer'?"

Now the box reacted, sprouting thin metallic arms and waving them a little frantically in the air.

"No," it said. "I wasn't finished. I was going to eventually get to the part where I told you about the central computer I designed, and how I had to download my consciousness into it to integrate the fleet's systems. I called it Central Engineer Reciprocation Virtually In Computer Embodiment."

Link raised an eyebrow.

"That's a long name," he said.

"Or 'Cervice'," the robot added, "for short."

Link felt his brow arch even higher, as he thought back.

"Service?" he repeated. "Only with a 'c'?"

"Consciousness integration technology was only getting started," the mechanical thing said, "when the fleet was being built. Synthetically created people were not afforded the same rights as organic humans, and their status as thinking and feeling individuals was questioned from the moment they began to think and feel. All artificial intelligence on our world had certain safeguards, the kind of safeguards that would prevent even the smartest computer from making decisions for a fleet of ships containing organic life. I had to—"

"I'm going to help you," Link said, cutting it off again. "I saw inside the mind of the man whose body I am inhabiting, and I watched him do terrible things. I want to stop him from hurting more people, or killing them. Tell me what I need to do."

The metal box rolled backward two feet, then rolled forward one.

"Don't be flippant about it," it said. "The Admiral is a very dangerous man, more cunning than anyone I have ever known. You will have to be very careful, and strong. It is entirely possible that one such as yourself will not be up to the task at hand."

Link tried to push himself back in his chair, indignantly. He forgot that the seat was attached to the floor, and all he managed to do was spin about a bit and wobble a lot.

"Listen," he said. "I didn't ask for this. You are the one that needs help. I'm trying to be nice, and a good person, and do the right thing. This could all be a dream, as far as I know. And what do you mean, 'one such as yourself'? You don't know me, or what I've been through."

He stared down the device, and thought about what it may have been through. Link wondered what it was like, to be an organic mind trapped in a network of alien circuitry; it couldn't be any more strange than inhabiting someone else's body.

The metal box remained unresponsive, and Link waited. He didn't know if he was staring down an opponent or waiting for it to speak, so he kept staring at it in the most intense way he could muster. It wasn't hard, with all the intensity crackling through the body he was in.

"I know everything you've been through," it said, at last. "The part of my mind that is computerized can sift through all of the information that is you in moments, and the part of me that is human can group the information in a way that gives me a complete and accurate profile of your life. Your days are shorter than ours, although we have adjusted to a schedule more like your planet's during our time in space. We live twenty to thirty cycles, before being evaluated for regeneration. Some live as many as forty cycles, if they are rejected. Your people live only three to five cycles, with no option for renewal. As a species, it's a wonder you have made it so far living for such a short period of time."

Link felt his shoulders sag, and his confidence evaporate. If this thing could flip through the files of his life in a few minutes, there was really no comeback to its assessment of him.

After a pause, the voice continued.

"That being said," it noted, "you're what I've got."

Link brightened, a little.

"I put out a call," it went on, "and you are the only being that answered. Perhaps it is some genetic resemblance to The Admiral, or some aspect of your chemical or mental makeup that tuned you in to the frequency I sent out. And perhaps..."

The thing paused, and Link was more frustrated than ever that it had no face for him to read between its words.

"Perhaps this is your purpose," it finished. "Perhaps you have been brought here for a reason, what your people would call a destiny and what my people would refer to as your purpose. Just as I am The Cervice, I who used to be The Engineer; you are The Link, and you will correct the path of The Admiral. Your purpose may be tied up in our history, and your story may be told for generations to come. That is how my people learn, by distilling great events and people into parables that—"

"The Link," Link echoed, trying not to laugh.

Cutting the robot off seemed to be the only way to let it know that he wasn't nearly as interested in its people's or its planet's history as the rambling collection of metal seemed to be.

"So," he said, "you used to be human? Or a person of your race?"

There was no pause, and no emotion in its voice.

"Our word is surely different," it said, "as are all of our words. Your word for 'human' translates to my word for our race for us both, before you speak it."

Link nodded.

"And man?" he asked. "Is the word and concept of that the same? Were you a man? Or am I being sexist?"

The machine paused again, and emitted a sound that Link thought might be a mechanical noise for laughter a few million light years away.

"Sexist," it said. "You are that. You think women are better than men, or at least better than you. That makes you a self-deprecating sexist, but a sexist nonetheless. I see that it is your society's conditioning that has caused this. You seem to be programmed to ignore the differences between men and women, while our people celebrate those differences. You even seem to have programmed yourself to act less like a man than you feel compelled to, in order to please women and society in general."

Link coughed, and glared at the box.

"You didn't answer me," he said. "Are you a man or a woman?"

The box was annoyingly unresponsive for a moment, and Link almost pressed it further in a louder voice. His hand twitched, and he had to remind himself that he didn't really want to see the rolling box explode.

"Our third sex is as rare as yours," it said, "and as special. Many of our leaders have been members of the third sex, which your world has categorized endlessly while shunning it as completely as your lack of mention of it does. Nonetheless, I was what you would call a man. Now, I have no sex at all."

Link nodded.

"I don't have sex anymore either," he said. "Not since July."

The machine may have been looking at him in some specific way, or thinking that it was; from the outside, it just looked like an expressionless box. Without a mouth to speak through, even its words seemed mechanical.

"You may be exactly what we need," it said. "Someone who knows so little that you can act without thinking. Surely the universal mind would send us nothing less than what we need."

It paused again, and once more Link got the feeling that it was eyeing him in some way that he couldn't see due to its lack of actual eyes.

"And perhaps," it added, "nothing more."

An indignant response leapt to the mind that was not his, but Link found that he was no longer in control of its lips. He stuttered, incoherently, while the body he was inhabiting collapsed in on itself a little. Then he felt the frame straighten, and grow increasingly unfamiliar; and the next thing he knew, Link was spinning through that timeless vortex to be plunked back into his own body.

He woke with a start, and looked at the bedside clock.

As many hours as had passed, they felt insignificant in light of the conversation he'd just had. Link was a young man, in a world where nearly everyone died long before they could leave the legacy they were born to leave. Lying in bed, the feel of comfortable sheets somehow made him feel smaller, diminished by the decision to pursue any degree of comfort in what little time he had. The rest of his night was spent in disturbed wakefulness, and he tossed and turned without rest.

TEN

Steve was already in his cubicle when Link arrived at work the next morning. He was going through a stack of papers, sorting them into three separate piles. As Link stepped into the space, Steve looked up and smiled.

"Morning," he said. "I got the day's work from your inbox. Since I don't have your passwords, I didn't want to get started on any of the actual entries. I know I could log into your computer with my password; but you should get credit for all the work I do while you're training me, don't you think? Did you have a good night? You look like you had quite a night. Maybe you should go get some coffee. I'll keep batching these according to the program we need to use, so we aren't jumping back and forth all day."

No matter how many times Steve deluged him with multiple waves of words punctuated by a handful of questions, Link could not get accustomed to the overwhelming onrush. All he seemed able to do was pick one or two of the several things Steve had said and do his best to respond before the next series of waves hit him.

"Morning," Link said. "Coffee sounds great."

He shuffled to the break room, stopping before going in. Sherry was in there, alone; and he saw her first. Link considered turning around and heading back to his cubicle, before she could spot him; instead he walked into the room, holding his breath despite his conscious attempt to breathe normally.

Usually he had coffee he had brought from home, enough to last until most everyone else was done getting their morning cup. On the rare occasion that someone was in the break room when he finally went for a refill, he tended to glue his eyes to the bulletin board on the wall until they had vacated the space. It gave him an excuse to avoid engagement, although nothing interesting was ever posted on the board. Mostly it was the same stuff it had always been, notices about what the state and federal minimum wages were and who he was supposed to call if he saw something inappropriate going down in the workplace. He had read nearly every boring and soulless word countless times. The Christmas party flyer was pinned to the board as well, and he smiled when he saw it.

"Good morning, Link."

He tried not to sigh when he heard his name from her lips, and Link put on his most deliberately expressionless face as he turned to the sound.

"Good morning, Sherry," he said, calmly.

There was no way she could hear his heart pounding from across the room, even if Link was convinced that the sound was louder than his voice had been. She stood there looking at him, as if she was waiting for him to say more. He smiled finally, and thought of something.

"Did you have a good night?"

Sherry nodded.

"I did," she said.

Something in her face and voice was very serious. Link felt his eyes narrow, as he tried to figure out what it might be.

"Sorry," she said, abruptly.

Sherry broke the eye contact, and stepped aside.

"You're here for coffee, not to talk to me," she said.

Lifting her own cup from the counter, she threw him one last sideways glance as she slipped from the room. Her voice drifted back to him, as he selected a mug from the cupboard.

"Have a good day, Link."

Back in his cubicle, Steve was crackling with energy and bubbling over with words.

"No offense, Link," he said, "but you really don't look so hot. Why don't you go ahead and sign in, and just look over my shoulder every once in a while. You're a great teacher, you know. I think we covered pretty much everything yesterday. If you want to kind of chill, and answer the occasional question, I got this. How does that sound? It looks like you didn't get much sleep. Did you have trouble sleeping? Or were you out late? You really should get your rest, you know."

By the time Steve had finished talking, Link had signed in and moved his chair out of the way. He took his phone from his pocket and began to surf the internet, looking for all the usual information and people that didn't seem to exist.

Steve could be quiet, when he was working. Although Link got the sense that he wanted to strike up a lot more conversations than he did, Link's pointless web surfing was still interrupted intermittently throughout the day by one inane set of questions or another. When it was about work, he would set down his device and either reach over to the keyboard or point at what Steve needed to do while explaining. The other questions he mostly ignored, or answered flippantly without looking away from the screen in his hand.

Toward the end of the day, Steve brought up having a drink after work in much the same manner as he had the previous afternoon. Link told him not tonight, again; with no good reason, again.

"Should I stop asking?" Steve said.

Link replied without looking at him.

"Nah," he said. "We'll go for a drink, one of these days."

Steve responded, a hopeful lift to his voice.

"Maybe tomorrow?" he ventured. "It is Friday."

Link kept reading the information that was not informing his situation at all on the little lighted screen. Once more, he responded without looking up.

"Yeah," he said. "Maybe tomorrow."

It hit him while he was reading something about electrical fields and how they extend indefinitely into space somehow. Link realized that he may have come up with an idea, and in the next moment he realized that the idea might actually impress the robot consciousness that he was trying to help. The first realization made him want to leap from his chair, and shake his fist triumphantly in the air; the second made him want to let out a loud whoop.

Link did neither of those things, but whatever subtle shift in his posture or expression did happen was enough to catch Steve's attention. He glanced at Link, and smiled.

"Good news?" he said.

"What?" Link let his smile fall, replacing it with a slight frown without looking over.

"Nah," he said. "I mean, yeah. Sure. Whatever."

They sat there like that for a few more seconds, Steve searching Link's face while politely avoiding looking at his phone. Link continued to scroll, and read, and keep the frown locked in place.

Link watched the clock on his phone march slowly through the last hour of the day, and tuned out even the questions that he normally would have answered. All he could think of was the feeling of twin pills sliding down his throat, and his consciousness spinning through space once more. He was nearly jumping out of his own skin, quietly, at the thought of getting home and jumping into someone else's.

ELEVEN

He wasn't sure if their sleep schedules were starting to sync up or if his increasingly earlier bedtime was giving him the time he needed. Link stepped into The Admiral's body while it was still asleep, and found it easy to take complete control. Immediately, he went to the log book and sat down before it. Instead of recording anything, he flipped back through the scrolling virtual pages until he figured there were about a month's worth of entries ahead of him. Then he started reading, and trying to paint some mental picture with the few notes that he could somewhat understand.

Something clicked, a few pages deep, and images began to flood his mind unbidden. Rather than having to piece together the completely alien life written in obscurely personal shorthand, he found that each entry began to act as a key to some doorway in the mind he was inhabiting. He flipped back further than he had to begin with, and started over. As soon as he reached the end, he flipped back even more. Scenes played out in his head, more fully fleshed out each time he read a given entry; and by the time he had caught up to today the third time Link was trembling.

He stood abruptly and began pacing, trying to order his whirling thoughts and still his shaking hands. Part of the wall disappeared as he stepped in front of it, opening up onto a hallway that was already beginning to swell with morning striders. Link moved away from the opening, and called out quietly.

"Cervice," he said. "Can you hear me? Any way you can close that opening? And maybe send one of your metal minions to—"

The wall took shiny shape once more, and a smaller spot opened up at the opposite side of the room. A faceless hunk of metal rolled out, and Link sighed.

"Can't you send something else?" he said. "Like, maybe one of those humanoid robots that I saw you inhabit while you were talking to The Admiral?"

Without a word, the metal box reversed its course and disappeared into the wall again. Less than three seconds later, the same opening appeared that he had just asked it to close; before Link could protest, a woman stepped into the room. She was striking, and confident in the way she entered. Link gathered his wits, and came up with the most intelligent thing he could think of to say.

"Uh..." he said.

She was looking at him with a wry smile, and Link was doing his best to figure out why. The dark hair that cascaded over her face in the most alluring way only drew his attention to her flawless flesh, and the electric green of her eyes. Her clothes seemed little more than a second skin, and it was all he could do not to let his gaze stray to the contours of her body as she edged closer to him. A lighted strip of fabric made a collar at her neckline, and matching cuffs ended at her wrists; otherwise she was covered with a material that moved along with her every subtle gesture. Although she was shorter than him, and considerably smaller, Link could not have felt more intimidated. His inability to talk to beautiful women, coupled with the completely alien environment, had him more flummoxed than ever.

Link made sure his mouth wasn't hanging open, and that his eyes didn't wander inappropriately. It was really all he could do.

"The Admiral does not behave this way around women," she said.

Her voice was as smooth and contoured as her body, and as flawless as her skin. Something about the way she spoke made him cock his head to the side, and look closer.

"Especially when she is an android," she added.

Link sighed, and nodded at the opening behind her.

He began to speak, in a normal tone.

"Would you...?"

The opening closed, and they were alone together.

"You need to learn some things about this fleet," she said.

Link nodded, and put his hands on his hips. He let his natural feelings take over, and glared at her with that intense anger that was flowing so freely in him whenever he saw the robot in any form.

"And you," he said, "need to figure out a better way to teach me. I've already got The Admiral freaking me out with all the stuff I'm learning about him; I don't need you preying on my weaknesses on top of everything else. You need to be explaining this place to me, not springing impossible tests on me and giving me a bad time when I don't pass. So I don't know anything about your world, and you somehow know everything about mine. There are only so many ways you can make that point, and time is wasting while you do."

The entire time he was speaking, she kept a twisted little smile fixed on her lips; it made Link feel even more annoyed, and he kept talking because he didn't feel like stopping.

"Like every morning," he said. "You all go walking through the corridors, together. What's that all about? How do you tell one corridor from another? And how do I tell a person from a robot? And how does The Admiral treat beautiful women? Or robots?"

She winced each time he used the word 'robot', and Link couldn't help but notice.

"What?" he snapped. "What am I doing wrong now?"

Suddenly her expression shifted, and the twisted sarcasm of her smile gave way to a pitying frown. Before Link could raise his voice again, she spoke. Her voice was gentle, quiet and measured.

"You are right, of course," she said. "The highly advanced consciousness does not benefit in any way from making light of the situation others find themselves in. I do apologize."

Link shook his head.

"Well," he retorted, "you've got a funny way of saying it. Also, you have a lot of explaining to do."

"I do," she said. "Would it help if I switched back to a clearly inorganic body? You seem to have some sort of difficulty relaxing around the female form."

Resisting the urge to rankle, Link shook his head.

"It's fine," he said.

He looked her up and down, since he knew it wasn't a she.

"Maybe next time," he added.

She watched him watching her, the bemused smile creeping back onto her face.

"Looking for seams?" she asked.

Link shrugged, returned his eyes to hers.

"We don't use that word," she said. "Since the rights of artificial intelligence became an issue, we don't call any example of it a robot. I am an android in a form like this, but only because I am connected to a central interface. Independent intelligences of an inorganic nature don't even like that word, anymore."

"Okay," Link said. "Well, what do you call them?"

Crossing her arms and shrugging her own shoulders, she smiled.

"People," she said, simply. "We call them people. Artificials, if a distinction must be made. Many would argue that there is no need for such distinction, and our society would change if the rest agreed."

Knowing what she was, Link tried to convince his mind that she was not what she appeared to be. She was not even a she, if she was inhabited by a consciousness that used to be a man. It was all very confusing, and he walked a slow circle around her. In a way, he was sort of looking for seams; he couldn't get his mind to digest what it knew, and see the beautiful woman in front of him as some kind of machine.

"Now you're acting like The Admiral," she said.

She had spoken without turning, and he was behind her. Link realized that he must have accepted what she was to some degree; he would never inspect the slightest curves and crevices of a woman he had just met like this. Without taking his eyes off her perfectly rounded backside, he responded without really responding.

"You have relationships with each other?" he asked. "Humans and...uh, organic people and artificial people?"

He was finally coming around to face her, and found himself staring into her bright green eyes with a frankness he had never turned on another human being. No wonder he had thought they looked electric; they were electric.

"We have relationships," she said. "In fact, a part of our fleet is dedicated to the study of interspecies relations. We may meet others in the vast expanse of space, and we need to know how to overcome the prejudices that seem to inherently plague interspecies relationships of all kinds."

Link burst out laughing.

"You have sex with robots?" he said. "In preparation for one day having sex with aliens?"

She shook her head.

"Our race is far beyond that," she said. "Our young are created and cared for by the midwives, until they are old enough to serve. We only have sexual relations for pleasure, and many of us opt to use our chemical control bands to eliminate the desire altogether. Interspecies relations are not forbidden, but they are frowned upon by many. It would seem that you share their prejudice."

"Prejudice?" Link frowned. "Interspecies? We're talking about robots here, Cervice. Machines. It's not that I have some moral objection, especially looking at you. I just can't understand how you can have a relationship with a thing like that."

It was her turn to laugh, and shrug.

"A thing like that?" she said.

She pointed at him, with a breathtaking sneer.

"I wouldn't have a relationship with a thing like that," she said. "Most artificial intelligences stick together, like people do. They...we don't consider organic life to be on our level, since they clearly aren't in so many ways. Like your people, mine have been working with the same organic hardware for hundreds of cycles; but our creations get smarter constantly, doubling their former capacities in every regard several times in a cycle. I am one of the few who has experienced what it is like to be both, and the only one who knows for real; and I must say that everything I once was is easily contained in what I am now."

She moved closer to him, and Link felt his eyes go

wide. He could smell her, she was so close; and her scent was as perfect as the rest of her. Her odor wasn't flowery, or earthy, or detectably artificial. Strong but subtle, it was the smell of womanhood distilled over centuries by precisely mathematical machines. It made no difference that he knew that, as it filled his nostrils; Link felt his heart begin to pound, and a flush begin to creep up his neck. He wondered if she was manipulating her chemicals, and that smell, to create exactly the effect he was feeling.

"The question here," she said, "is not whether or not a man like you would want a woman like this one. It's whether or not she would have any use for you. Artificials are as prejudiced toward humans as humans are towards them, and perhaps more rightfully so. I can hear your heartbeat, and monitor your organic systems with very little effort. I know you desire this body, even knowing what it is and who resides inside of it. Do you know how amusing and repulsive it is to watch you battle your own inner animal and inner human, in a fight to see which is the least detestable to both of us?"

Rather than crumple further under her assessment of him, Link thought back to something else she had said. He frowned, pointed at the lighted cuffs and collar.

"Are those chemical control bands?" he said.

"In a sense," she nodded. "We have three, to monitor different systems. Organic people generally only have one, unless they have an issue the regenerator can't resolve."

Link felt his own wrists, and neck. They were bare.

"The Admiral refuses to wear one," she said. "It's why you can't help but respond to this form, even when you don't want to or think that you should. He handles it better than you, but he won't just do what everyone else does and let his desires be completely conscious."

Link nodded.

"It seems more authentic," he offered. "As nature intended."

She waved a hand, to take in the entire scope of their surroundings.

"Where is nature in all of this?" she said. "The Admiral suspects that I will find out something damning about him if he is part of the network, because I probably would. His body chemistry surely drives the awful things he does, and I have been tempted more than once to reveal those actions to the crew. They would surely vote to force him to submit to examination and network immersion. For his own good, of course."

As he was about to comment on how creepy and invasive that sounded, Link let his mind drift back and felt his flush go white.

"I forgot," he whispered.

One of her eyebrows shot up, in the most organic way.

"Forgot what?" she said.

Link crossed his arms, to keep one of his hands from reaching for his weapon. The urge was suddenly harder than ever to resist.

"I had an idea," he said. "I read through his log book, to try and figure out what he was up to. It gave me some kind of serious peek into his mind, into this mind."

Link tapped the head that wasn't his, even if it felt and looked like his.

"That's wonderful!" she exclaimed.

Moving even closer, she looked up at him with appraising eyes that seemed to like what they saw. His heart was already pounding, and now it seemed to skip a beat.

"It's not wonderful," he said. "I'm supposed to be on my way to torture someone to death right now."

TWELVE

When she reached out and put her hand on his arm, Link felt a tingling thrill run the length of it. He didn't have any way of knowing if it was his natural reaction to feeling a woman's touch, or if there was some kind of actual subtle electrical current involved.

He didn't have time to ask.

"This is an opportunity," she said. "We must seize it."

Two urges battled within him: the urge to pull away, and the urge to move closer to her. It was a stalemate, and he stood still.

"No way," he said. "I know he was a big supporter of yours, but this is too much. I can't rescue the guy. I don't know enough about your weapons, or the layout of the ship, or how to—"

"Hush," she said.

Her voice was so calm and soothing, and her hand was patting his arm gently. Link was fairly sure it was a programmed effect, but he appreciated it nonetheless. He hushed.

"That's not what I meant," she said. "You would reduce or eliminate our chances of effectiveness if you did something so obvious. The team leader was only useful to us so long as he held his position. This is an opportunity to see who he gives up, and warn them immediately. Here, take this."

Her hand went behind her, and reappeared holding a small object. It looked like a large seed or a very small clove of garlic, made of metal. He took it from her.

"What's this?" he said. "And where were you stashing it?"

"Stick it in your ear." She smiled, patted him again. "I'll be able to hear everything that is said in the room, while it's happening."

The urge to back up finally won out, and Link felt his eyes go wide as he stepped away from her.

"While what is happening?" he asked.

It only took her one step to close the distance between them, and place her hand gently on his arm once more.

"The torture," she said. "You've got to do it, whatever The Admiral was going to do, and intercept the information he's looking for. After it's over, you've got to head to his quarters and record the events in his log."

She smiled, and there was a twisted kind of triumph in the expression that Link didn't find comforting at all. Either she sensed it, or her programmed instincts were better than those of most humans. She patted him again, and he felt much better.

Link thought back over what she had just said, and shook off the contact. Another step backward put him too close to the wall for him to back away any more.

"I'm not torturing anyone," he said.

Looking back at the wall behind him, checking to see if it had gotten any closer or further away since he had last looked, Link eyed her warily.

"I can't do that," he said.

He started shaking his head doggedly back and forth, muttering those two sentences under his breath over and over. Stepping closer, she put her hand on his shoulder. She spoke, softly.

"You'll save so many others," she said. "I'll alert the people that he puts at risk by naming them, before it's even over. I'll tell you who got somewhere safe, and what to write in the log book. This will be a giant win for us."

Link had stopped muttering, but he wouldn't meet her eyes. She shook him, a little, and he glanced up.

"Link," she said. "This is why you are here."

He held her gaze, even as he shook his head.

"I thought this was a dream," he said. "I'm still not so sure it isn't. If my unconscious mind is trying to see if I am willing to torture someone, I think the way to win that one is to not do it."

Even when she shook her head and frowned, she was beautiful.

"If this were a dream," she said, "then it should be interpreted as a message from some aspect of your deeper self, alerting you that it is at war with some other part of your deeper self. You would be seeking to eradicate the part of you that is cruel and unfeeling, represented by The Admiral. Your unconscious would surely test your mettle in such a conflict, and see if you are up to serving your own highest good by doing something you might otherwise interpret as terrible."

He was up against the wall at this point, and she had her hand on him again already.

"That sounds like something The Admiral would say," he protested. "It doesn't even make sense."

She smiled, and patted his shoulder.

"Of course not," she agreed. "Because this is not a dream. Your mind has not created this scenario, The Admiral did. This is a hard thing, and I understand that. But if you walk away, half of the fleet will die. Maybe more. Please stay here, Link. Please help us."

Link sighed, and nodded. He had a good look at the thing she had given him, then he put it in his ear. It expanded, to fit in the most perfectly comfortable way, without dulling or amplifying his hearing at all. He sighed again.

"Tell me how to get where I'm going," he said.

Her touch was gone, as she turned her back to him. In a few steps she had reached the opposite wall, and part of it disappeared. Link did his best to keep his eyes off the shifting contours of her body, and the alluring sway of her dark hair.

"I'll do better than that," she said. "I'll show you."

The hallway was still cluttered with people, and he whispered fiercely so they wouldn't hear.

"Wait," he said. "Aren't we enemies? Should we be seen together?"

As she turned, Link dragged his eyes upward to meet hers. Her lips didn't move, but he heard her speak just the same. He felt his eyes go wide, in surprise, until he remembered the thing he had put in his ear. That was where her voice was coming from, a device placed perfectly to sound in his ear like it did when she spoke.

"This body is not mine," she said. "It belongs to a woman that is sympathetic to the cause, but not openly so. It is not strange for you to be seen with her, unless you continue to behave as though you have never kept company with a beautiful woman before."

She pivoted again, and strode into the hallway. As Link began to follow, her voice came again in his ear.

"You can speak very quietly," she said, "and I can hear you perfectly."

Link passed a couple of people, walking together the opposite way, and smiled disarmingly at them both.

"Like this?" he said, under his breath. "Can you hear this?"

When she nodded, he could see her hair swaying with the motion. He stayed behind her, and kept his eyes on the walls and floor. The reaction that he had gotten from his friendly little smiles had him avoiding eye contact with others that passed. Less people filled the hallway than earlier, but they were all still moving at a pace just short of running. He noticed the bands of light on each of them, and how some had one and others had three. The people with a single chemical control band wore them wherever they pleased, and hung them from their bodies like jewelry. Most of them were on their wrists, while many were around their necks; Link only saw a few that wore the rings about their ankles.

Now that he knew, it was pretty clear who was what.

Telling them apart with any physical feature or mannerism would have been impossible, if not for the bands. The people were as youthful and healthy and flawless as the robots. It wasn't the first time he had seen it, but he hadn't taken particular notice of it. Making almost no sound, and moving his lips very little, Link asked her about it.

"Where are all the old people?" he said. "And why is everyone so..."

He searched for the word, watching more people pass out of the corner of his eye.

"Healthy," he said, at last. "Why is everyone so healthy?"

Link saw her shoulders shake, and heard her laughter in his ear.

"Our bodies are all like machines," she said, "both organic and artificial. We keep them properly maintained with foods dense in nutrients and daily exercise, and monitor them for problems. The chemical control bands take care of the rest, what little there is to take care of, until we reach the end of a cycle. Then we go to the regenerator, and begin our next cycle as youthfully as we began the last. That is why these people are walking, as they do every morning. A brisk morning walk every day has too many health benefits to ignore, so we pretty much all do it together."

He was glad he was trailing behind her, so she couldn't see the surprise on his face and chastise him for that too.

"What do you mean?" he said. "You are immortal? All of you?"

A slight shrug lifted her shoulders, and her words came in his ear.

"We weren't always that way," she said. "On our planet, we had a selection process for who would be renewed. Now, our numbers must grow. Unless someone has a valid argument for foregoing regeneration, we all go through it. Although we haven't been on this journey for long, everyone in the fleet who was eligible for regeneration has gone through it. We face a different population problem than we did before, and it is once again up to all of us to solve it."

She stopped abruptly, and Link nearly collided with her.

"Here we are," she said. "Your duty lies on the other side of this wall."

The complete absence of a framed doorway didn't bother him. Link could see the placard on the wall, so much like so many others he had seen as they walked. Instead of words, they all had simple symbols on them. This one had a picture of bars, crossing over each other: it was the holding cells. It brought the gravity of the situation down on his shoulders once more, and Link felt them sag.

"I'll be with you," she said, in his ear.

Link nodded, and faced the wall resolutely. An opening appeared, and he strode through it as confidently as he could. He was glad that his presence was expected, and that it was easy to follow the series of sudden openings in solid walls to where he was headed. The thought that he was breaking into a prison that he would end up in if he was found out did not escape his attention, but he tried to pay it as little mind as possible.

Too soon, he was standing before a man strapped to a chair. He looked like a different person, and Link had to peer closer to identify him by his features. They were gaunt and hollow, deep lines etched in his countenance by the pain he had been enduring. Link noticed the man didn't have a chemical control band on, and that it appeared as though he had not had any food or water since being strapped down.

Link glanced at the man behind the prisoner, sitting in a chair and watching the other's bent frame twist further with each turn of the knob. The torturer met his eyes, and nodded.

He cranked the knob, and the prisoner cried out.

"You are in control here," Link said.

The words surprised him as much as they did the other man, and Link crossed his arms over his chest as he examined where they had come from. His greatest fear was not knowing what to say, in any situation that required words to navigate. While he had been searching, as he was accustomed to doing, something had slipped the simple phrase past his fumbling mind and through his lips. Link stepped aside, mentally, and let more words flow.

"You can end this pain," he said. "All you need to do is tell me who is plotting against me, and your suffering will cease completely."

The prisoner was tensed up, the whole time he spoke; when Link fell silent, he relaxed enough to look at him and answer. Link was as impressed with the attention the torturer was paying to the exchange as he was disturbed by the entire proceedings.

"You'll kill them," the man said. "After you kill me. I won't betray them."

Link laughed, unbidden and humorlessly.

"It's in your character," Link said. "You betrayed me. Actually, the only way to repair the damage you have done in betraying me is by betraying them. Give me their names, and I will set you free. I will give you a new assignment, and I will leave you alone. I give you my word, you shall have more freedom to move about unchallenged than any other member of this fleet."

Link motioned to the man with the device, and watched the prisoner begin to twitch painfully. Fresh beads of sweat appeared on his brow, and his eyes seemed to sink further into his skull.

"Or," Link said, calmly, "you can stay here forever. Cervice may have other allies, but so do I. My allies are prepared for war, while his are trained to avoid conflict. He is weak, as are his supporters. When he loses this battle, he will lose control of the fleet. I will remove his consciousness from the central computer, and there will be no chance of this happening again. During that, and forever after, you will stay in this room. You will receive the minimum amount of sustenance required for your survival, and you will be brought to the edge of death as often as you can handle it. If we take things too far, we will revive you and bring you to the edge of death again. You will receive regeneration treatment when it is called for, so that you can live forever in this state."

Another subtle gesture, and the man began to convulse in response to the machine's signals. Link felt a part of him wanting to cry out, and tell him to stop; another part of him thrilled at the sight, and had him leaning forward. He felt his own heart pounding, and his fists tightening painfully at his sides; Link bit his lip, to keep from shouting with agony or delight.

Link waved his hand, and the prisoner relaxed once more.

"Make your choice," Link heard himself say. "Either way, this is the last time you will see me."

The man was pouring sweat, and gasping for breath. Link wondered if the prisoner had even registered his words, as he pivoted in place and headed for the wall where he had come in. An opening appeared, and he strode toward it.

A voice called out behind him, withered and beaten.

"Wait," the prisoner said. "The person helping the most is a woman that they are beginning to call The Speaker."

Link stopped, and smiled. He spoke without turning.

"The Speaker is dead," he said. "That is an elected position. And one that has been eliminated. She is treasonous, as are the people calling her that."

As he spun slowly, he saw that the prisoner was nodding in agreement.

"Of course," the man said. "I see that now. I will tell you all of their names, and I will accept your offer of redemption and mercy."

Link nodded. He turned his attention to the man with the device.

"No more pain," he said. "Leave us."

Pleasure had lighted the torturer's eyes while he was turning the knobs; a twist of slight irritation replaced the expression as he set aside the device and stood next to his seat. He gave the prisoner one last long look of disgust before he moved toward the gap that remained open in the wall.

"Don't go far," Link said, as he passed through the opening. "You'll be escorting this man to his new post when we are done here."

This time, the man's disgusted stare was aimed at Link. It was the last thing he saw, before the opening in the wall closed behind his exit. Link listened to the names, paying as little attention to the information as possible. It wasn't hard, since none of the names meant anything to him. Cervice was listening, and would do what it had to do.

When the man was finished, Link stepped to the wall once more. It opened, to reveal the torturer patiently waiting in the next room.

"Take this man to the main airlock," Link heard his own voice say. "And give him more freedom to move about than anyone in the fleet."

As one man's face went from disappointment to thinly veiled glee, the other's morphed from relief to terror.

"Admiral," the prisoner said. "You told me I would get a new post."

Link nodded.

"I did," he said. "Your new post is in research. We have never monitored a chemical control band when it was attached to an otherwise uncovered living being exposed to space."

The prisoner's face fell even further, if that was possible.

"Uncovered?" he echoed.

Link was torn between feeling sick over the words coming from his own mouth and taking utter joy in them. The joy won out, and he smiled as he nodded at the prisoner once more.

"Your next post," he said, "is a recently created assignment. The only way I could end your suffering, give you more freedom than anyone in the fleet and give you a useful post is to come up with a new one. You will float in space alongside the fleet, as a caution to those that would endanger our continued survival. It is perhaps the most important position ever created, and you will serve in that capacity forever. Do try to live as long as possible out there, so we can learn as much as we can from your passing. And try to smile. You will be out there forever."

On his way through the opening, Link stopped but didn't turn. He spoke one last time, while the prisoner could still hear him.

"Forever," he said again, "or until your body drifts away."

THIRTEEN

She was there waiting, when he stepped through the last sudden opening and into the corridor. Across the hall, he saw her watching him as he emerged. Link motioned to her, and she looked around confused.

"Help me," he said.

Link felt himself sagging visibly; it took every bit of effort he had to subvocalize, instead of cry out to her. He watched her cross the space between them, and heard her voice in his ear despite a total lack of movement in her lips.

"Link?" She sounded shocked. "Is that still you?"

As soon as her hand fell on his arm, he started feeling better again. She led him with a gentle push at his elbow, and he let her. They passed through the corridors together, her guiding him and talking soothingly and soundlessly in his ear.

"You did so well in there," she said, "I thought The Admiral took over, while you were talking. You must have learned a lot, reading his log. You sounded so much like him. It was disturbing."

Link nodded, feebly.

"He did take over, in a way," he muttered. "Those were not my words. Those were not my ideas."

An image came to his mind, of a frozen body floating in space with nothing but a lighted bracelet on one of his wrists.

Link shuddered.

"I think I'm going to throw up," he said.

The hand on his arm began to pat him lightly, as it guided him.

"I don't think you can make me feel better," he said.

She gave his elbow a little squeeze, and another series of pats. Despite his protestations and unwillingness to admit it, Link did feel a little better.

"You'll be fine," she said, without speaking. "Try to keep your voice down. You did great in there, you should be very proud of yourself. Think of the people you saved, not the one you sacrificed."

Link nodded, trying to bring up a thousand beautiful immortal faces he had never seen in his mind to blot out the image of the one he had.

"I still think I'm going to be sick," he said.

Her hand kept guiding him, as her voice continued to soothe him.

"You'll be fine," she said again. "Just a little further, and you can write down what you need him to remember in the log book. His lack of memory will cast further doubt on his own mental faculties, as he sees events that he can verify and that have been recorded in his own hand but he has no memory of. This is a big win."

Link frowned, shook his head.

"You never said anything about messing with his head," he said. "That seems kind of unfair, to deliberately make him doubt himself."

The squeeze was harder this time, and Link stiffened.

"Keep your voice down," she reminded him. "This is war, Link. We must press every advantage we can get. The electromagnetic field that we generated to surround the fleet is not doing the job it was designed for properly.

People's memories are beginning to slip, and several cases of acute amnesia have occurred. Everyone has come back, so far; but the lapses are getting worse, and all of us are in danger of being affected."

Link made sure to whisper, such that his lips barely moved.

"Even you?" he asked.

"Especially me," she said. "I don't just rely on the field for continuity, like everyone else; I monitor it, and maintain it. If I forget to do that..."

She trailed off, and Link saw the small sea of faces behind his eyes begin to twitch and cry out. It was his imagination, a daydream within a nightmare; but somehow that made it seem more real than any of it.

A gentle pull on his elbow slowed him, and they stepped sideways into his chambers together as the wall opened up to admit them. Link went to the chair, in front of the log, and slumped into it.

"Hurry," she said. "We don't know how much time we have left. You've never kept control of him this long."

Link sat up straight, and lifted the stylus from where it sat on the desktop. It lit up as he did, and he touched it to the flat screen under the last entry. She began to speak, and he began to write. All of his will was bent on imitating that strange shorthand, and keeping himself from vomiting on the record. When her voice began to sound like it was coming from very far away, Link turned in the seat and looked up at her.

"I can't...uhhn, mharrg," he said, clearly.

She bent, and reached out to him. Link thought she was going to cup his head with her hand for a moment, and kiss him. Instead she retrieved the device from his ear, and lifted him easily and bodily from his seat. Link sagged in her arms, his motor functions dwindling rapidly. His head lolled onto her shoulder, and he could feel her breath against his ear.

"Hold on," she whispered. "Don't let him back in until I'm gone."

The response he tried to give her sounded a lot more like words in his head than it did coming through his lips. It was enough, at least to tell her it was still him and that he heard her. She placed him on the bunk, and lowered him gently into the position he had woke up in.

Link saw her lean in, one last time.

Again, he thought she was going to kiss him. He could neither lean into it nor turn away, had he wanted to do either of those things.

Once more, he was wrong. She got close enough that he could feel her breath on his face, and she spoke.

"Thank you," she said. "You are The Link, and I thank you."

She stood abruptly, turned and walked briskly through the opening that appeared in the wall. Link watched her, since his eyes were pointed that way and he couldn't seem to move at all. When the wall took shape behind her exit, Link let his eyes drift closed.

The spinning confusion was a welcome loss of his sense of self, and Link swirled in the nothingness with the hope of never returning to either of the two worlds that battled for his soul and his consciousness. A hard heaviness hit him when he was just getting used to oblivion, and his eyes flew open to stare at his own ceiling.

Link launched himself out of bed, his hand over his mouth. He made it to the toilet, but just barely. The mixture of bile and goo in the bowl captured his eyes and nose at the same time, and he vomited more thoroughly on top of it. Link flushed, and threw up again while the water took the whole mess on a slow spiral to wherever such things go.

Closing the lid, Link collapsed on the floor and inched his way from the bath mat to the cold tile. He lay there for some time, face pressed into the hard coolness, thinking in a detached kind of way how disgusting it was to lay on even your own bathroom floor. After awhile, he realized that he needed to go to work. It took all he had to drag himself through his morning routine, and to the job. Link wondered, not for the first time, how many things he could do that took all he had to do them before he just couldn't do any more.

FOURTEEN

Steve began laughing as soon as he saw him.

"Link, good morning," he said, "I thought I told you to get some rest. You look like you didn't sleep at all last night. Oh, hey; and you smell like a distillery. Why don't you sit down, and let me get you some coffee."

Link waved his hand, collapsed into his chair.

"Don't be silly," he said. "I haven't had a drink in days."

Link pulled his chair up to the keyboard, started typing. He cast a sideways glance at Steve, when the other man didn't move.

"Coffee does sound good," he said.

Steve nodded.

"I'll get some for both of us," he said. "And you might want to change your shampoo. It smells more like spring break than spring fresh."

Link waved his hand again, and turned back to the screen. He finished logging himself in and slid away from the computer, removing his phone from his pocket before the seat had stopped rolling. A sound came from behind him, and he spoke without pivoting toward it.

"You're in the system," he said. "You can set my coffee over here."

Steve didn't follow the direction of his voice, and no

mug was placed on the desk beside him. Putting down his phone, Link spun halfway round in his chair to see what the holdup was.

Sherry was standing there, half in and half out of his cubicle. She looked as well put together as ever in a form-fitting skirt suit. The jacket was tailored both to fit her and to accentuate the slimness of her waist and the rounded curvature of her breasts. Instead of a tie or a scarf, her buttoned blouse was open to hint at the presence of cleavage without really giving away any of its secrets. Only one of her legs was visible, tentatively stepping into the space, and dark stockings began where her skirt and heels ended.

Link's gaze wanted to go everywhere but her face, so that's what he looked at. He tried to smile, and not notice the dark half-circles under her eyes that were not quite covered by what little makeup she wore.

"Good morning, Sherry," he said.

She smiled, and straightened where she stood. As she began to move more completely into the cubicle, she spoke softly.

"Good morning, Link," she said. "I was wondering-"

"Hey, Sherry," Steve said, poking his head in behind her.

Sherry started, and glanced at him as he sidled past her with two steaming cups of coffee.

"Oh," she said. "Good morning, Steve."

Steve was setting down the coffee cups, his eyes on the task at hand. Sherry moved back, so more of her was out of the shared space than in, and watched Link carefully until Steve looked up. Her gaze drifted then, to the flyer he had pinned up on the textured wall.

"I was just checking in," she said. "Making sure you guys are both still coming to the Christmas party."

Opening his mouth to reply, Link shut it when Steve leapt in.

"It's awful nice of management," he said, "to invite me to the party my first month on the job. It seems like a great opportunity to get to know everyone, and I really appreciate you guys thinking of me. I'll be there, you can bet on it. Thanks again, it really means a lot."

Her eyes found Link's briefly while Steve was talking, and she looked back at the flyer immediately. When he was finished, she nodded and gave him a friendly smile without making eye contact.

"Sure, Steve," she said. "Great, I'll see you there."

Now her eyes found his, openly and deliberately. Link thought he saw something in them that hadn't been there before, some sadness or happiness or tiredness that gave them a soft satisfied glow.

Link nodded.

"I'll be there," he said.

The delightful pressure building in him while Link held her eyes was too much, and he turned to Steve.

"Ready to get after it?" he said.

Steve nodded. After a final glance in Sherry's direction, he pulled his chair closer to the computer screen.

"Alright, then," Sherry said. "I'll let you guys get to work."

Link could feel her for several moments after she spoke, still lingering half in and half out of the work space. The feeling that made him want to spin his chair about and say more was the same feeling that would turn his words into an awkward mishmash if he did, so he kept his back to her and pretended he wasn't breathing in the sweet subtle scent of her.

When she had finally gone, Steve nudged him.

"See?" he said. "I told you."

His daily internet surfing had already begun, and Link only felt the nudge and heard the comment from the corner of his mind.

"Hmm?" Link muttered. "Told me what?"

Steve's rolling chuckle was punctuated by the clicking of his fingers on the keys. Link couldn't even tell him to get to work, since he knew better than anyone how little attention it took to do his own job.

Another nudge got him to look up, and catch Steve grinning.

"She's got a thing for you, man," Steve said. "How are you not seeing that? Did you see how she brushed me off, and was all intense when you were talking? Come on, man. You think she's going around, checking personally to see if everyone is making it to the party?"

Steve's fingers were hovering over the keyboard now, and they were looking directly at each other with very little space between them. Although they hadn't become besties in the last couple days or anything, they had often ventured into conversational territory that was not appropriate to shout across the shared office space that lie beyond their partial walls. Their exchanges had taken a habitually quiet tone, and the last one had been no different.

Link opened his mouth to speak, and shut it when he heard another voice over the wall. He was grateful for their customary low volume, even as he tried not to burst out laughing with all his voice.

"Hey, Jenny," Sherry said, loud enough for them to hear over the common wall. "I'm just checking in, to see if you're still planning on making it to the party."

The other woman's answer was drowned out, on their side of the divider, by the almost pained sounds of the two men trying to keep from exploding with laughter. When they finally got over the fit, and its aftershocks, Link went back to peering at his phone with the utmost intensity. A minute later, he nudged Steve and spoke without glancing up.

"Yeah, Steve," he said. "I do think she's checking in on everyone."

For the rest of the day, very few words passed between them. Link was cooking up a new plan, and making it a point to check the unnecessary timepiece he wore on his wrist. Steve took the hint, and didn't ask about a drink after work or what his plans might otherwise be.

Besides, sharing would be ridiculous. How could he explain to Steve that he needed to get home as soon as possible, to take the regularly prescribed dose of a pill that was transporting him to a fleet of star stragglers so he could ride along unnoticed with the fleet's admiral? If Steve believed him, it would take too long to tell it all; the value of his friendship would be thrown into question by him believing such an unlikely story, and the telling itself would be rendered pointless. If he didn't believe him, word might get around the office or Steve might think he was blowing him off. Doing anything sincere was sure to get him into a situation he didn't want to be in, so Link put his whole self into his disingenuous act and got himself home and in bed by the time the sun went down.

FIFTEEN

The solitary pill had the same effect as before, and Link found himself staring out through eyes that he couldn't move or shift. He noticed right away that The Admiral held his body differently than Link did, and walked with a markedly longer gait. Watching the internal workings of the man's mind was as fascinating as watching their subtle outer manifestations. Link found himself studying The Admiral's speech patterns, and trying to get the hang of his cadence, before he realized what the man was saying.

"We've got to get some handle on this," The Admiral said. "The electromagnetic field generator is Cervice's chokehold on all of us, and there's no telling how much further he'll endanger everyone to take me down and seize control."

Link was reeling from his good fortune, and the stark statement. It took him a few long disoriented moments to register what The Admiral's eyes had been showing him for some time. The person he was talking to was a striking young woman, her blonde hair tied back in a severely feminine style he had never seen before. She wore stripes of makeup, blended with her skin tone everywhere but around her eyes. They were ringed tightly in black, with long slim tails trailing to each of her temples. The deep set of her eyes and the dark shadowing of her makeup triggered a remembrance in him, and Link realized he was looking at the woman that had been strapped to a chair and tortured last time he saw her.

He couldn't express his shock at her transformation, or bumble through some awkward set of words meant to compliment her that actually put her off considerably. The single pill made him a passive observer, a silent witness in another man's mind. All he could do was watch, and take note of exactly how The Admiral could be expected to act around a beautiful woman.

"Sir," she said, "even the artificials are beginning to worry, due to the lapses in memory. Many of them are entertaining the notion that Cervice is causing them, and using them to gain more control of the fleet. Where they were once publicly behind him, they are now pointing out his possibly quite human motivations. You were right, people are beginning to realize that he is not one of them anymore; at the same time, artificials are hesitating to call him one of their own as often as they were just a short time ago. We have more allies today than yesterday, and some of them could play an important role in putting you in control of the EMF generator."

The woman was standing up straight, simultaneously rigid and relaxed. Her body's posture spoke of a military mind, but her eyes were steadfast on his for some other reason. Link felt The Admiral smile within, while making it a point to keep his features expressionless. The mind he was inhabiting was surprisingly quiet, and clear; the only real sense he was getting of the other man was the way he felt inside, and how carefully he kept any outward indication of it locked down tight.

Finally, he spoke; only Link and The Admiral knew that he had something else he wanted to say.

"Limit everyone's interactions," he said. "Remember that we are always at risk of being under observation, and make it a habit to assume that Cervice has more information on us than we have on him."

She laughed, surprising all of them.

"Sir," she said, "I doubt that."

Her smile lasted a split second longer than it should have, and The Admiral spoke as it faded.

"Make it a habit," he said, "nonetheless."

The woman nodded, the picture of seriousness once more.

"Of course, sir."

It was The Admiral's turn to smile slightly, and say what he had been thinking quietly all along.

"I will be in my chambers in an hour," he said. "You are most welcome to join me there."

She flushed slightly, and smiled. Without waiting for a response, The Admiral spun on his heel and strode away. Link rode along, wondering if an hour was really the same as an hour to them; and if meeting someone in their chambers had similar connotations in both worlds. If this guy could go from torturing a woman to romancing her in a few short days, Link really had no hope of acting the way he did around anyone.

As preoccupied as he was with another man's thoughts, Link once again failed to notice what the eyes he was looking out through were approaching until they arrived. It was that same wall screen he had seen on his first visit to this reality, showing the expanse of space stretching out into infinity before them. The sight would have taken his breath away, if it had been his to take; The Admiral was calm and quiet approaching the view, and his breath continued to cycle with the same measured rhythm that it always did.

The Admiral moved as close to the transparent or projection wall as he could, until the slowly approaching stars in the distance filled his entire field of vision. Riding along, Link felt both his own awe and the other man's; it felt as though it must be true, that no matter how many times a person saw this kind of thing it would never fail to strike them as truly and breathtakingly awesome. For once, Link could relax and let the other man's thoughts be his own.

A sound behind them surprised Link, but The Admiral simply sighed. The sigh was internal, where he kept most of his reactions, and only he and Link felt it. They turned together, slowly, toward the noise.

It was a life-sized collection of metal, cast to be humanoid but unmistakably inorganic. The dull grayish luster of its outer layer moved and flexed like skin, covering every part of it other than its eyes. The eyes were blue sparks of electricity that went white when it spoke. Its mouth opened, and moved; the insides it revealed were the same dull metallic hue as its outer layer.

"Admiral," it said. "I would have words."

The Admiral laughed, but only inside the head that Link was occupying. Rather than retort sarcastically, he nodded.

"Cervice," he said. "Have them, then."

The robot shifted, and stood up straighter.

"We have worked together, in the past," it said. "One could argue that it was only by working together that we built this fleet, and launched it."

The Admiral nodded.

"One could say that we worked well together," he said. "For a time. Until you betrayed me, and attempted to gain control of the fleet. If one were to consider the big picture, rather than conveniently selected parts of it, one would surely have to concede that we didn't work so well together overall."

It put its hands on its hips, in the most inanely human gesture it seemed it could muster. The robot spoke again, and Link noticed there seemed to be more emotion in its voice than there had been in The Admiral's.

"Surely you see," it said, "how you clearly betrayed me, and not the other way around. I mean...you killed me!"

This time the laugh was audible, and genuine; The Admiral let it come to a natural rolling stop before he replied.

"And yet," he said, still smiling, "here you stand!"

The Admiral crossed his arms, and pushed the smile down with a fierce frown.

"It's hard to take you seriously," he said, "when you come to me as actual service components. Why not inhabit a regular body, like the other artificials? You must have access to several."

Its head moved in negation, and the metal opening that could be called its mouth seemed to frown.

"So you could kill them?" it retorted hotly. "Or identify them, and torture them for information?"

Link felt one of The Admiral's eyebrows go up, and he leaned slightly forward along with him.

"Who said anything about torture?" he said.

The Admiral didn't wait for a reply.

"It wouldn't be so easy," he said, "to do this, with an actual person."

The Admiral's hand went to his hip, and Link didn't even see the thought fly by that told it to. One moment he was standing there with one eyebrow arched, relaxed and at ease; in the next, he had the device he kept shooting things with in his hand, and it was shooting this thing too.

Very little smoke rose from the collapsed contraption, and one of its eyes still had a spark of blue in it. The Admiral shot it once more, and two more times after that, before holstering the weapon.

Link watched mindless knee-high drones wheel out of panels that slid open in the wall, and saw them clean nearly all the pieces before he felt that familiar spinning lure from his own world. He felt The Admiral blink, and shake his head; and then he was gone into the darkness.

SIXTEEN

Link's eyes were only open for as long as it took to seize the nearby bottle, and take another pill. The glass of water by his bedside was old, and stale; he didn't care. He put one down, then the other, and lay back down to go to sleep. Not a single glance went to the clock, or registered what time of day it must be by the light outside; the only actions he took in his own world were purely perfunctory, and done to get him back to the other.

Just as time seemed to pass slowly between realities, it flew by while he was disengaged. Link was both disappointed and relieved to find himself, as The Admiral, saying goodbye to the woman he had been talking to earlier. They were together in his chambers, her hair was loose and flowing freely about her shoulders, and the makeup under one of her eyes was smeared in the most strikingly suggestive manner. She stood near the part of the wall that opened up to the rest of the ship, gazing up at him and smiling softly.

"How do I look?" she asked.

Neither of them made physical contact of any kind, although it was clear they had recently engaged in plenty of it. Link heard the thoughts in the head he was sharing, and couldn't believe the man was not considering telling her she looked beautiful or gently dabbing at the smeared bit of coloring under her eye.

"You look fine," The Admiral said. "Make sure no one sees you leave."

He turned his back to her, and moved to the log. The sound shifted in the room, as the opening appeared; a moment later it was silent again, save for the dull rumbling that could be heard anywhere on the ship. Link watched him make his strange shorthanded entries, watched the thoughts that played across the landscape of the other man's mind even more closely, and rode along with him to a shared mealtime.

The food they ate was surprisingly similar to what Link was accustomed to, other than the lack of sweetness or strong flavoring. He could taste it as well as the man whose mouth was chewing it, and tuned out the mild but delicious sensation as easily as he did. The Admiral's thoughts were on his plans and his people, while Link's wandered the full spectrum of fascination. Everything from the utensils they ate with to the trays they ate from to the food itself was familiar and alien all at the same time, and he was silently delighted to discover that the trundling robot Cervice had used to communicate with him earlier was indeed for clearing and storing trays.

The Admiral ate in a slow and considered fashion, as did everyone in the shared eating space. Conversation did not fill the room, any more than the raucous sound of utensils banging on trays. No one behaved in a particularly relaxed or hurried fashion, and he was no different. Link felt the calm of the others like it was a palpable field of energy, permeating both his host and his own deeper mind with a shared tranquility.

Instead of being disappointed that the second pill

only gave him a glimpse of the man saying goodbye to his paramour and a spectator's seat at mealtime, Link told himself he was gaining valuable knowledge by just getting more familiar with the other man's thoughts. When he woke again, there was no consideration of where or when he was; all that mattered was losing as little time as possible in riding along for a day in the life of The Admiral. He took another pill, without bothering to wash it down with water or refill the empty glass from earlier, and jumped right back into the other man's skin.

Next was a meeting where a slew of terms Link didn't understand got thrown around quite a bit between a lot of people he had never seen. They seemed to be weighing the dangers of courting an asteroid field with the benefits of mining a rich variety of ore from the selection it offered. The Admiral was pointing out how much they had buffered their fuel reserves already, and how unlikely it was that they would find another opportunity like it soon if they set about adrift. A few were vocally opposed, arguing that some ships had been destroyed and many more damaged since the fleet had begun interacting with it. Others pointed out that they had detected a new gravitational presence, which could indicate safer mining conditions relatively close by.

Link did his best to follow the conversation, only to find himself counting the lighted bands on the other people attending the meeting and being pleased that he could tell who was what.

The arguments were all made in a measured and considered tone, and no insults or berating words came from either the people or the robots. Cervice was in attendance, the only clearly artificial being in the room for anyone who didn't know about the bands. He surprised Link, putting forth only reasons for them to stay, and complimenting

The Admiral on his clarity about the situation. Link had difficulty determining who each person was, or what duties they performed, in the stalwart quiet of his host's mind. Only when their shared eyes fell on Cervice did the other man react emotionally, and he kept those reactions from showing to anyone but Link.

At one point, it was all too tempting for him to call Cervice out. He was making a point about the ships that had been damaged or lost, and how each had been a calculated risk that had ended in zero casualties. The robot gestured toward him, and nodded in his direction.

"The Admiral has made many hard decisions," the robot said, pivoting slowly to catch every natural and artificial eye in the room. "They have all been correct, in the end. We must rely on his ability to make those hard decisions, and continue to lead the fleet unflinchingly in the direction of our continued shared purpose. So long as lives are not being lost, everything we do lose can be replaced due to our proximity to large quantities of every element imaginable. If we leave behind this opportunity in search of another, we could be drifting a long time before we find it. Situations exist in which a gravitational field of the nature of the one we have detected could indicate something other than available resources, or even less tenable mining conditions than those we are now dealing with. Better the devil we know..."

When his lighted artificial eyes found the ones Link was looking out of, he felt a rage boiling in him that almost made sense. If Cervice had so much confidence in The Admiral, why go to such great lengths to undermine him? His hand twitched at his side, but stilled as he respectfully returned the robot's nod.

Link rode with him for as long as he could, until he felt irresistible tendrils of darkness begin to claw at the edges of their shared mind. He was pretty sure that his host consciousness was heading to his chambers for a sleep cycle, but he wanted to make sure before he let the darkness take him.

They were both surprised to find the woman he had engaged with earlier, waiting outside the part of the wall that would disappear with his continued approach. He ushered her inside, and crossed his arms over his chest. The wall took silent shape again as he spoke.

"How long have you been out there?" The Admiral demanded. "Who saw you?"

She shook her head, and smiled.

"No one saw me," she said. "And I haven't been waiting long. I came as soon as we figured it out, because I knew you would want me to."

He nodded, arms still crossed.

"Alright," he said. "Then tell me."

She bit her lip, as if to keep from laughing.

"We found a way to shut down the central system," she said. "I also figured out how to turn it back on, without rebooting The Engineer. Admiral, sir, we've figured out how to kill Cervice and save the fl—"

He took her in his arms, surprising her and Link alike with the sudden movement. She reacted immediately, wrapping her arms about his waist and fervently returning his passionate kisses. Link reacted in the next moment by giving in to the darkness, and slingshotting back into his own lonely body.

SEVENTEEN

Link hesitated, two pills in his hand. He didn't want to jump into full control while The Admiral was with that woman, any more than he wanted to miss his window of opportunity to warn Cervice of their plans. He decided to put the pills back, get up, and draw a fresh glass of water. His phone was in the kitchen, on mute, and he turned it over on the counter and pressed the home button.

It lit up, showing him several things he hadn't expected all at once. The date was all wrong, the time was too late, and there were messages waiting to be viewed.

Link looked at the window, as if the sun would be up for some reason not indicated by the digital time stamp. The curtains were dark, as was the world beyond. When the phone's light faded, he tapped the button again. Fingerprint technology sensed his authenticity, and the lock screen turned into his home screen.

The messages were from Sherry, and there were two of them. The first had come in Friday night, and was nothing more than five question marks. The second was the same, a series of question marks; it had come about an hour into the party he had missed on Saturday.

It was past midnight, which was why the date display said 'Sunday, December 25'. That meant it was not just the worst time to call or text; it was also the worst day of the year for the kind of message he might send. Of course, that didn't stop him from starting to compose one.

'Sorry,' he typed, then stared at the screen.

"Sorry what?" he muttered under his breath. "Sorry I find my dreams more interesting than you? Sorry I slept through the party, I was busy trying to save the world? Well, not the world; but a world. Or a bunch of people, anyway. They probably only exist in my mind, but just in case they are real I want to dedicate my life to living one of theirs. It will probably only be for a little while, then we can get on with having some kind of relationship that I can screw up in an entirely different way."

His hand was shaking, poised over the single sorry word. The thoughts were whirling in his head, going in circles top speed in a way that seemed to pain him in a very real fashion.

Link deleted the apology, and had another look at her series of punctuation marks. He tried to scroll up, and couldn't. Confusion furrowed his brow, as he tried to remember deleting the exchange they'd had the other day. Thinking back hurt too much, and even keeping his brow furrowed caused a real and tangible ache in his head.

The phone went dark with another touch, and Link set it on the counter. He needed coffee, to make the growing pain subside. The thought of it made his stomach grumble, reminding him that he likely needed food as well. What he really needed was a way to go back, and start at the beginning with Sherry; although if he had that ability, Link would spend his whole life just going back. It was likely he would never make it through an entire day.

With a sigh, he turned on the brewing machine and listened to it warm up while he got a mug from the cupboard. It still wasn't ready when he was, so he looked at the question marks Sherry had sent him one more time. No new information leapt out from between the characters, and Link darkened the screen and set it down again. He made a cup of coffee, and took it into his living room to sit in his easy chair and stare at the silent and blank television.

The coffee began helping his head pain immediately, while also clearing the muddled track of his racing mind. Link attributed the dull metallic aftertaste to the fact that he had gone so long without eating. His thoughts continued to turn in useless circles, beating him up for sleeping a day away and reminding him that he already had enough personality quirks to create a life of loneliness without adding this to the mix; but at least the spinning uselessness didn't physically hurt any longer.

His thoughts went to Cervice, and The Admiral; they only stayed as long as it took to remind himself that they should be in a sleep cycle, and he should have plenty of time to rest and eat before he needed to get back to their world. Right around the time that he finished drinking the coffee, Link realized that he was still feeling rather exhausted. He pulled the lever to kick back the easy chair, stretched out and yawned.

"I may be sleeping more than ever," he mused quietly to himself. "But I feel more wiped out than ever, too. All I need is some real sleep, in my own body, while they get theirs in space. Then I'll go back. Then I'll help, however I can. Then I'll..."

His voice drifted off as he did, and Link felt those tendrils of darkness reach out to pull him to another world. The pills were still working in his system, and he didn't realize it until he opened his eyes to a bank of alien technology.

The Admiral wasn't sleeping, after all. He was kneeling next to a metal wall, where part of it had disappeared to reveal what looked like an access panel. Instead of colored wires and clumsily exposed connections, the device behind the wall was a visible electrical field of some kind. What few connections there were appeared to be transparent glowing tubes of glass that burrowed deep into the base of the simple clump of metal; it seemed to be generating the field, while acting as a pedestal for the projection. Other than the lights pulsing through the transparent tubing and pouring into and out of that miniature stage, all of the activity he could see was happening in the image that floated above it.

A voice to his right startled Link; The Admiral did not share his reaction. He turned to the sound, almost smiling. It was the woman he had been with earlier, of course; his top flyer, his recent prisoner, and his more recent lover. Link chided himself for being a fool, thinking they would sleep on such big plans. He realized what he had been looking at, through the other man's eyes, as her words registered in his mind.

"That's it," she breathed, turning to him. "That is the central computer core; and that thing floating above it is Cervice's brain, essentially. We need to shut it down, and have our little friend here fire it back up."

The Admiral's eyes went to where she indicated, following the wave of her hand. A simple contraption on wheels sat next to her, no more than knee high. It had four appendages, long arms that ended in intricate metal claws or clusters of interchangeable tools. Dull lights glowed on the otherwise featureless front plate, the only hint that the thing was anything other than a mindless hunk of metal.

"We've only got a few minutes," she said.

The Admiral's gaze found hers again, and he nodded.

"Cervice is unaware of our presence, and will be staring at a recorded loop if it looks down this hallway," she went on. "This is one of the few robots on the ship that it can't control, but that isn't all it does. It also generates its own electromagnetic field."

Link could feel the other man wanting to grin, and even leap to his feet and let out a victorious shout; he didn't, though. Calmly, The Admiral asked a quiet question. There was no smile on his face when he did, or even the hint of one.

"How big is this field?" he said. "Will we be in it?"

She frowned slightly, and shook her head.

"No," she said. "Just our little friend. He'll reconnect the central computer, and engage the EMF generator, while bypassing Cervice altogether."

A heavy sigh tried to find its way through the body he was inhabiting, and a feeling of fear tried to tighten his belly. The Admiral breathed through it, and stoked the fires of the rage within him; the feelings subsided as he spoke again, still keeping his voice down.

"So we'll lose our entire identities for a few minutes," he said, "and rely on that thing to bring us all back? That seems like a lot of faith to put in one machine. I don't like the thought of our lives being completely in the hands of one of them."

The last word sounded like a curse, the way he said it. Her eyes drifted from his, to the pulsing electrical field set in the wall. Blue and white light cast an eerie artificial glow over her features, and deepened the lines around her mouth when she frowned.

"I agree," she said. "But we have no other option. Either we depend on this one for the next few minutes, or we hand our world over to that one. It doesn't seem much of a choice, to me."

Link was sure the only reason he was here was because he had taken enough pills earlier in the day to send him here. Without taking two right before going to sleep, like he usually did, there was absolutely nothing he could do but quietly panic deep inside the other man's mind. He had no voice, to shout or even think loudly; from this side of the glass he seemed to stand on, he could see and hear everything The Admiral experienced with absolute clarity; but it was one-way glass, and no amount of soundless pounding or silent shouting could touch that distant alien brain.

All he could do was watch, as the woman reached out her hand and put it on one of the glowing tubes of lighted connectivity. Her eyes went to the robot at her side.

"Are you ready?" she said.

The lights on its front plate brightened visibly, all four of its appendages moved slightly, and it trundled forward a few inches on whirring wheels.

She turned to him, and she was biting her lip slightly.

"Are you ready?" she said, once more.

Against all of his useless protestations, despite his entire weakened will trying to pour some kind of control or lack of it into the other man's limbs, Link felt his head nod.

She tugged, and everything went dark.

EIGHTEEN

Link sat upright in his easy chair, startled further back into reality by the thunk of the footrest loudly finding its way home. His heart was pounding, and it felt unnatural to sit still. A moment later he was pacing the only small strip of his living room carpet that he could pace comfortably on, and not feeling any more at ease than before. He saw himself from the outside, for a brief moment of embarrassed clarity; rather than cease his static wandering, he dismissed the viewpoint and started talking to himself.

"It wasn't even real," he muttered. "It was all just a dream, a dumb pointless dream. I maybe had a shot with a real girl, and things were going great at work. My mind had to sabotage me somehow, to keep me living the lame life I'm supposed to be living. I mean, Cervice? What kind of a name is that? And how smart can you be, if you get outwitted by a guy that looks just like me?"

He kept pacing, and muttering, changing subject midstream.

"Forget all that noise," he said. He straightened his posture and slowed his pace, although he did continue walking back and forth mindlessly. Believing in what he had muttered seemed to be the key, so he said it again.

"Forget all that noise," he repeated. "It's time for me

to get it together. I've got no business trying to help some alien race that my mind made up, especially if its going to turn what little of a life I still have upside down. I don't care if it's Christmas morning, or will be soon. I'm going to text Sherry, or maybe call her. There must be some explanation I can give her, that won't make it sound like I'm some kind of loser than prefers his stupid dreams over real life."

All through his shower, he thought about it. While he brushed his teeth and gargled mouthwash, he thought about it. He thought about it while he made another cup of coffee, and the whole time he was drinking it. As he brewed another cup, Link had to admit that it was hopeless. There was no excuse that would explain away his behavior, and no reason for her to give him another chance when he hadn't really had one to begin with. Both of his worlds had terminated in dead ends, on the same night.

He didn't know what constituted celebrating in the fleet, but he thought The Admiral must be engaged in some version of it. That, or he was roaming mindlessly through the corridors of the ship. Either way, curiosity got the best of him once he finally got around to filling his belly with some lump of substances that he neither heated nor tasted. His body may have gotten used to him sleeping so much, or his full belly was drowning him in drowsiness; whichever it was, Link didn't have it in him to resist the pull of whatever version of unconsciousness awaited him.

The sheets were neither clean nor dirty, and he slipped between them in fresh pajamas. Link eyed the bottle of pills for a full minute, then shrugged and took two of them. He washed them down with water, set down the glass and closed his eyes before his head touched the pillow. The shocking familiar feeling of traveling without moving pulled him from his body, and plunked him once again into The Admiral's.

A new morning had begun, in the eternal night of space, and Link awoke in the other man's mind mid-stride. He had been walking alone, along with all the others, making an effort to look normal. Link took over the exact same task, falling into step without moving at precisely the same pace as anyone. From the corner of his eye he watched, to see if anyone was perhaps watching him from the corner of their eye. Nothing seemed to have changed, although he couldn't be sure what he was looking for. The Admiral felt as exhausted as Link did, but that made sense. He had been up all night.

He held an intention in his mind, and trusted his feet to take him where he wanted to go. Link was relieved and moderately impressed with himself when he found those steps leading him to The Admiral's chamber. The wall disappeared at his approach, and he went inside. As soon as the partition had reformed, he went to the log book.

No new entries had been written, and Link slammed his fist down on the desk beside it. He found the mirror again, and tried to stare deeply into the other man's eyes in hope of seeing his thoughts. All he got was a blank stare. His own blank stare.

Link sighed, and threw his arms up in despair.

"Cervice," he said. "Please tell me you can hear me."

The silence that followed was punctuated only by the dull rumbling that never seemed to cease or falter. Link felt himself cringe inside the other man's mind, felt a knot of hopeless anxiety twist more tightly with each moment that passed with no answer.

He stumbled to the wall, and it opened at his approach. The hallway beyond was nearly empty, and he moved along it with no thought of where he might be going. Now that something may have gone horribly wrong, Link was suddenly convinced beyond a doubt that this world was real. He was sure Cervice was dead, that thousands of people had depended on him to save them and he had let them down. Link wanted to run; he wanted to dash down the hallway, calling out for Cervice until he appeared somehow.

Instead he walked, hesitating at every intersection to cast his gaze as far down each corridor as he could. It was a ridiculous search, and Link knew it; if Cervice was still alive, he would have seen Link and come to talk to him as soon as he had begun to act strangely. Link started to move faster at the thought, walking at a panicked pace that suggested he may break out into a run at any moment. Moving without looking, chased by his own fears, he collided with a group of people as they came around a corner. He bumped into one of them, careened off and smashed bodily into another. Both of the people he had hit dropped something when he did, and by the time he stopped bouncing off them there were a number of items scattered on the floor at their feet.

Before he could apologize, all three of them tossed their own hasty apologies his way. He bent with them, to help pick up the fallen items, and they waved him away. One man and two women, all three smiled uneasily and extended another round of apologies while he knelt and began to pick things up. The items were foreign to him, pieces of carefully constructed metal that surely served some purpose that was beyond him. As he handed the last of them to one of the women, he smiled at her.

All three of them exchanged glances as they rose together, and two other people had walked by during the exchange. He heard them, whispering to each other as they walked away.

"Now I am getting concerned," the first, a human, said.

"I know," the artificial responded. "If The Admiral is starting to forget himself, maybe the EMF really is failing."

They drifted further away, as did their voices.

"Maybe he's just trying to be nicer," the first said.

The robot laughed, and said something Link couldn't hear. He turned his attention back to the group, noting that they were still busy exchanging meaningful glances. They were all artificials, though he could only tell by the bands.

"Admiral," one of the women said.

The other two looked at her, trying to hush her with fierce glances that did not give Link any hint as to what was going on. She shrugged, and went on.

"Sir," she said. "Are you feeling...like yourself?"

"Engia!" the other woman snapped, shaking her head. The man looked back and forth between them, then sighed and shrugged.

"Link?" he said. "Is that you?"

Link felt his own eyes go wide, but not nearly as wide as theirs. He blinked slowly, while he watched them exchange another round of meaningful glances, and finally he nodded.

"I'm Link," he said. "How did you know? Who are you?"

The woman that had started to speak was the one that answered him, leaning in and speaking in a hushed tone.

"There's no time to explain," she said. "Neero has something for you."

Shifting the burden he was holding, the man nodded. He reached behind him with the hand that was now free, and then held it out to Link. On his palm Link saw a device similar to the one he had put in his ear to talk to Cervice. He was glad the man had looser clothes, and pockets that Link could see. Even then, he hesitated before taking it.

Pinching it lightly between his thumb and forefinger, Link picked up the thing gingerly and inspected it for a moment. He put it in his ear.

"Cervice?" he said, hopefully. "Cervice, are you there?"

He exchanged glances with each of the three in the group before hearing a response.

"Link?"

It was a different voice, with the same cadence. The robot sounded both human and male, for the first time. Link felt the tension drain from his shoulders at the sound, and he nearly jumped for joy as the voice went on.

"I am not everywhere, anymore," Cervice said. "You must accompany the group you are with, to meet me. Do you have time?"

Link nodded, forgetting that Cervice had lost its omniscient eye for a moment. While he spoke, he nodded again.

"Yeah," he said. "I've got time."

He looked at each of the others again, in turn.

"Take me to Cervice," he said.

NINETEEN

Every corridor had looked pretty much the same to him, the first time Link walked the ship in another man's boots. Now he could see the subtle differences, and was fairly confident he could find his way back the way they showed him once he found a reference point. The whole way he watched for landmarks to burn into his brain, and spoke under his breath to Cervice.

"I thought you were dead," Link said.

"I am an artificial," Cervice responded. "We do not die. Nonetheless, I appreciate the sentiment."

Link heard him sigh, as if to negate his own observation.

"I suppose," Cervice went on, "I did die, in a sense. I am no longer a part of the ship, or the fleet. The central computer is functioning without my guidance, or my assistance. I was alerted of The Admiral's intentions before he disconnected me, and I downloaded my consciousness into a body."

Following the robots at a distance that would make them seem like they were going the same direction but different places, Link found himself getting curious.

"What kind of body did you choose?" he muttered.

The answer came back, after a considered pause.

"I didn't choose," Cervice replied. "My students actually chose for me. They constructed a body that is virtually indistinguishable from my original human form. When you see me next, I will appear as I did before I was murdered."

It seemed like a classically stupid idea, as far as Link was concerned. When hiding from an enemy, adopting any face you wanted sounded like a huge advantage. What kind of vanity had driven him, or his students, was beyond Link. He did not have time to comment, or question the decision; as he rolled the response around in his mind, the group came to a halt before him. They all looked around, appearing suspicious for the first time since he had joined them; then one of the women approached a wall, and an opening appeared. She motioned to the passageway it had revealed, and stepped back.

Brushing past them, Link entered the more narrow corridor. He heard the absence of sound, indicating that the opening in the wall had closed behind him; he pressed on, in the only direction he could. At the end of the hallway, another opening appeared. Link stepped through. Beyond was a simple room, small and sparsely furnished. A bunk dominated the space, and a small desk was set up just to one side of it. Someone was sitting at the desk, writing in a log much like The Admiral's. He had his back to Link, although he clearly had heard him enter.

"Uh…" Link felt awkward, unsure of himself. "Cervice?"

The man kept his back turned, and continued writing for another long stretch of seconds. When he was finished, he rolled the thin sheet carefully into a slim tubular shape. Opening the end of the stylus he had been using to write with by pinching the end lightly, he slid the rolled log into the barrel. He set it down, and pivoted in his chair.

"Link," he said, smiling. "I'm so glad they found you."

Link nodded.

"Me too," he said. "That was a happy coincidence,

running into your students like that."

Cervice raised an eyebrow, and Link had to remind himself that both the response and the eyebrow itself were artificial. The man wore three chemical control bands, but otherwise his was the most ordinary face Link had seen on the ship yet. Thought lines creased his forehead, and the eyes under them gleamed with intelligence; but no one would ever describe him as handsome, no matter how generous their assessment of him. Link found himself even more baffled by his choice of embodiment.

"Coincidence?" Cervice laughed. "That was no coincidence. Dozens of my allies have been instructed to keep a close eye on The Admiral, and approach him if he was acting strangely. There is a sense of desperation spreading, and you may be our last hope. The odds of you not being discovered by one of them were actually pretty slim."

Link arched his own eyebrow, organically.

"What's going on?" he said. "Doesn't he think he's already won?"

"The Admiral?" Cervice shook his head. "No. Getting rid of me is just the beginning. Now that I can't monitor him or the fleet, he can move on to what he plans to do next."

Link pressed him. "Which is?"

The robot gave a completely human shrug, and smiled.

"That's what we need you for," he said. "Look inside his mind, read his log book, ride along as a passenger. I know he aims to destroy the artificials, or at least separate us; what I don't know is how."

Link nodded.

"I looked at the log," he said, "before I came looking for you. There were no new entries. That was how I was unlocking his mind, and seeing his thoughts. I don't know how I can help."

A look of irritation came over Cervice's synthetic features.

"You have to try," he insisted. "Dig deep. Do you not see anything that belongs to him in your thoughts, or your feelings?"

Link resisted the urge to break out into a wicked grin.

"I still want to shoot you," he admitted. "More than ever, actually."

Shaking his head humorlessly, Cervice held out one of his hands. Palm up, he waited expectantly.

"What?" Link said.

"Your earpiece," Cervice replied. "We can't have The Admiral discovering it, or me."

Link removed the tiny device, set it in the robot's palm.

"I'll try," he said. "I'll come back, and watch what he does, and come find you. If I can still help, I will."

The communicator disappeared, and Cervice stood. Link noticed that the man looked frail next to the body he was occupying; he was still looking down at the robot, and his trigger finger was still itching.

"Thank you, Link," Cervice said. "Many lives are at stake, and I am convinced more than ever that you are our only hope."

He wanted to be in a corridor far from here when The Admiral returned to his body, preferably back in his quarters. Link began to turn, and find his way out; he paused, and looked the robot up and down one more time.

"That's what you really looked like, huh?" Link said.

Cervice nodded. Link went on.

"Why?" he said. "You could have looked like anyone, and wandered free on the ship. Why would you choose to be so...blatant?"

Cervice laughed.

"The ship monitors all life forms aboard," he said. "A new addition would have been a red flag, either way. I couldn't have just wandered around, whatever good that might have done, any more than I can now. The Admiral is in control of the central computer now, at least within its new limiting parameters."

The robot looked up at him, scorn clearly etched in his features.

"Link," he said, "your assumptions are so often erroneous, I don't understand why you continue to make them. Your understanding of our fleet seems to have decreased in the time you have spent here. I need you to pay attention, if you are to help us. Now that the central computer is working on its own, it is unable to make critical decisions. It's not just half the fleet that is in danger now; it's all of us. Please, take this seriously."

Link didn't understand what that meant. He also didn't feel like asking, and feeling even more stupid. The fact that he had slept away his entire three day Christmas weekend for the cause was not likely to be enough to impress Cervice, particularly since he would be back to work tomorrow and unable to return for some time.

"Tell me," he said. "Tell me what is going on. Why is the electromagnetic field generator so vital to everyone's memory? I mean, don't robot...ah, artificial brains work differently than organic ones?"

Link hoped a little curiosity would transform him from a pompous intellectual to a willing teacher. It had worked before.

Cervice nodded, pleased.

"Your own planet has sent people into space," Cervice said. "They soon realized that they needed to limit the time an astronaut spent in that atmosphere, as they began to experience both physical and mental difficulties after a relatively short period."

"Like memory loss?" Link said.

Cervice nodded once more.

"Like memory loss," he said. "Remember, that happened after a short period and not far away from your planet. Until you leave your own solar system, you retain some kind of connection with your home planet. That connection is electromagnetic in nature. When that connection is severed, the memory loss is instantaneous."

Although it didn't really make sense to him, Link responded.

"Unless you have a viable substitute," he said.

Cervice broke out into a synthetic grin.

"Precisely," he said. "And that's lesson enough for today. Go back to your world, attend your work ritual, and come back behind his eyes while he is plotting. Go now, Link, and do not think of this meeting until you are back in your own body."

No hand was proffered, and Cervice did not embrace him in gratitude or camaraderie. He simply turned his back to Link, went back to his desk and removed the log from its housing once more. For a moment Link just stood there. He stared at the robot's back, wondering whether he should say something or walk away.

Finally he sighed, and left the way he had come.

TWENTY

Somehow, after three days and nights of doing little more than sleeping, Link felt more exhausted than ever. He was not surprised when Steve made a comment, as soon as he walked into the cubicle.

"Whoa, buddy," he said. "I missed you at the party. Looks like maybe the party didn't miss you, though."

Link gave him a humorless chuckle, a single harsh note, and sat.

"I know," he said. "I couldn't make it. I had an awful weekend. Worst Christmas ever."

Steve's eyebrows shot up, and he frowned.

"Yeah?" he said. "What happened?"

The thought that Steve might ask a follow-up question had not occurred to Link, when he was waxing dramatic. Now he shrugged, and avoided making eye contact.

"Oh, you know," he mumbled. "Just not feeling well."

Steve was nodding dramatically.

"So I can see," he said. "You might want to see about taking some more time off. How many sick days have you used?"

Link laughed, and waved his hand.

"We don't get sick days here," he said.

Still nodding, Steve frowned again.

"Sure we do," he said. "I just got hired, remember? They went over all that stuff with me. Everyone accrues one sick day every quarter, even new hires like me."

Link was already standing. He looked down at Steve.

"How do I look?" he said.

"Honestly?" Steve winced. "A little awful."

Link grinned.

"Perfect," he said.

Without so much as a goodbye, he swept out of the cubicle and across the sectioned space. Marching directly into the payroll office may have been more to the point, but that meant walking by Sherry's office. Link took the circuitous route instead, and got there eventually. He tapped gently on the door before entering, although he knew it was another office filled with cubicles. A lone counter stood on the other side of the door, the only piece of furniture he could see that wasn't a flimsy wall. Behind it was a woman, with a cheery smile.

"Hi," she said. "Can I help you?"

Link's eyes roamed the floor, the walls and finally the top of the counter. He kept his gaze averted as he spoke, as if looking at her wrong might put a curse on all his future paychecks.

"Uh, yeah," he said. "My name is Lincoln Nash. I was wondering...do I have any sick days?"

Of all the things he considered she might do, Link was not prepared for what happened. He thought she might laugh at him, or stick her nose in the air and tell him sick days were only for important people, or announce that if he didn't want to work then he didn't need to have a job. Instead her smile widened, her fingers clicked quietly on her keyboard, and she nodded with her eyes still locked on the screen between them.

"Actually," she said, "you have four unused sick days."

Her eyes shifted from the screen, and she met his gaze.

"You know," she said, leaning forward a little, "if you don't use them, you lose them. You'll carry one of those days over to next quarter, but the others drop off at the end of the year."

Link frowned, his eyes still on hers. He looked around the office, to see if anyone else was listening in. Every other person in the room was either completely absorbed in their own work, or hidden behind cubicle walls. He coughed, unconvincingly, as his gaze fell once more on the woman that had been helping him. He coughed, again.

"I'm not feeling so well," he mused.

Her smile never faltered. It was still there when she nodded along with his words, and responded.

"I thought you might say that," she said. "You better get on home then, Mister Nash."

"My friends call me Link," he said, automatically.

Her smile faded, as she looked back at her screen.

"I'm sure they do," she said, flatly.

Link had been dismissed. He didn't mind; it was the sort of dismissal he had been hoping for.

"I'll probably need the rest of the week," he added.

Without looking over, the woman nodded.

"I kind of got that impression," she said.

Making sure to keep his shoulders drooping and his countenance downcast, Link exited the office and moped his way to the exit. Once in his car, he slumped behind the wheel and plastered a grimace on his face. He didn't let himself relax and smile until he was well on the way home; even then, he kept checking the rearview like he was afraid someone would chase him down and drag him back to his drab office space.

Finally home, Link calmed himself by changing the sheets and pacing the living room. He eyed the bottle of pills every time it was in view, as if he was afraid it would leap across the room and somehow force him to take one. As much as he felt like it was the right thing to do, Link hated the thought that it was something he must do. His life had always been defined by his ability to do as little as possible; having any kind of calling was too much pressure for someone who expected so little of himself.

After he had done everything he could think of to do, Link found himself staring down the bottle as if he was challenging it to a duel. He though of all the reasons why he should just chill for the rest of the year, and let the aliens and the robots both at work and in space deal with whatever came their way. Link even considered tossing the bottle in the trash, or flushing the pills down the toilet in a more defined gesture of finality.

In the end, Link gave in to his fate. He donned his pajamas with the slow awkward movements of a poorly programmed machine, put one of the pills in his mouth, and chased it down with a swig of water. Crawling between the sheets, he let himself hope that he wouldn't be jumping into any gruesome torture sessions or intense sex scenes.

And then Link was gone, spinning and shifting through space in that twisting way that he could never get accustomed to.

TWENTY ONE

His luck could not have been better.

The Admiral was attending another meeting, and Link recognized many of the faces surrounding him when the other man turned his head to look around. Of course Cervice wasn't there, embodied. He was the present topic of conversation, however. One man was speaking, and Link felt The Admiral's answer formulating long before he had finished.

"We need Cervice," the man said. "I believe our efforts should be focused on finding out what happened to him, and trying to restore him. The fleet cannot function as it was designed to without Cervice."

The Admiral interjected, before anyone else could respond.

"There is a way," he said. "A way for us to continue mining and resume our voyage when it is time. Cervice spoke to me, about what we must do if he was ever compromised."

Several others made a motion, as if to speak; The Admiral went on, paying them no mind.

"Cervice gave his life for the fleet once," he said. "Perhaps he did so again, in his own way. We all know he was looking into the problems with the EMF. Am I the only one that has noticed those issues disappeared when he did? I would contend that Cervice found a way to fix the problem, and the answer meant his electronic demise. Let's not waste everyone's life trying to get inside a mind none of us can understand. Maybe he became the electromagnetic field, and is with us in a way we can't grasp. Whatever he did, it stopped the memory problems; perhaps that was his ultimate service."

Link couldn't believe how eagerly some of the men and women present began to nod their heads. He noticed most of them had only one chemical control band, and that the few artificials present were exchanging suspicious glances. None of them were nodding, or smiling like the others.

"It sounds like just the sort of thing Cervice would do," one woman offered, tentatively.

The nodding heads bent more deeply, and a quiet murmur of assent found its way from one end of the room to the other. Nodding with them, The Admiral continued.

"We must act fast," he said, "or his sacrifice may be for naught. We are drifting in space, unable to continue onward or mine for resources. Cervice performed the vital function of bridging the gap between human and artificial consciousness, and was able to give sentient machinery the ability to act even when lives are at stake. Without someone serving that unique purpose, the fleet cannot proceed as it was designed to."

One of the artificials in particular was glaring openly at The Admiral. Since he made it a point to notice it, Link did the same. Neither of them was surprised when the woman leaned forward, and spoke.

"And what is your solution, Admiral?" she said. "Would you download yourself into the central computer, and dictate every move the fleet makes?"

The Admiral shook his head, keeping a calm and

composed expression locked on his face. Spreading his hands, he spoke soothingly.

"Kera," he said, "your teacher always suspected me of nefarious intent. Just think, if we had listened to her we would be on a dead planet, burnt to ash and gone forever. I'm afraid she poisoned you against me. I have no such plan, or intent. Cervice designed the interface specifically for his consciousness, according to him. Anyone that tried to duplicate his results could be killed. I have no reason to doubt his assertion. I certainly have no desire to give up my humanity."

The woman had been slowly slinking back into her chair as he spoke; when he said that, she flinched visibly.

"Then what do you propose we do?"

The voice came from one of the men who had been nodding with much enthusiasm moments earlier. Link could feel The Admiral waiting for the exact right moment to respond, watching some heads already beginning to bob in advance support of whatever he said next.

"We must separate the fleet," The Admiral announced. "The mining and scout ships will hold all artificials, while all naturals will inhabit this main vessel or their smaller community crafts. In this way, the vessels that can be piloted by humans will be operated manually. All crafts that require sentient artificial life to operate them will house only artificials."

Another robot spoke, rising from his chair as he did.

"We are to take all the risks?" he demanded. "We are supposed to keep mining, and scouting? And somehow, we're all supposed to fit in those cramped ships? You know they aren't made for comfort, or even for adequate housing."

"Of course," The Admiral cut in, "it would only be a temporary measure. We would be depending on you to come up with a new interface, and to select the candidates to take over this vital role. Any comfort we can extend you would be given freely, even if you choose to stop all mining operations due to your situation. Scouting would of course be suspended, as we all work together on this problem."

The artificial was still standing, and it seemed he did not want to sit down without adding something more.

"We work together," he said. "From separate ships. This is segregation. We have come so far; do we really wish to leap backward?"

He cast his electric gaze around the room, and found very few friendly eyes. Shaking his head, he took his seat once more.

"When Cervice was The Engineer," The Admiral said, "he and I stood on opposite sides of that very issue. I feared that we would be putting our fate into the hands of uncaring machines when he proposed the fleet initially, and I resisted his efforts to make it something that could be run entirely by an artificial intelligence. When he became that artificial intelligence, all of my fears and concerns and prejudices fell away. I deeply respected him when he was alive, but I never respected him more than when he became Cervice."

The Admiral took a step toward where the artificials were clustered. Link felt the other man's inner delight when the two that had spoken moved back visibly in their seats. On the surface, he smiled at the entire assemblage. The smile was disarming, the way he meant it to be.

"We need you," The Admiral went on. "More than you need us. Don't think I don't know that. I know you can tolerate difficult living conditions better than we can. I know the least among you makes the best of us look weak and frail by comparison. I know you will keep mining because you know what is best, and you always do what is right. If anything happens, I want you to be able to leave us behind. Navigating manually will surely be inevitably lethal for the rest of us, if we have to attempt it. I am trying to make sure we are not all lost, if our solution is not rapidly forthcoming. You will need the mining ships in that event, more than comfort."

Now all the heads were nodding, and the only voice in the room that was raised in dissent was Link's silent cry. Even The Admiral was unaware of him, and the anguish he was feeling within the other man's triumph.

"Do we need to vote?" The Admiral asked.

The tide turned, and all the heads began moving in negation. A few voices erupted, charged with excitement.

"We'll fix this," one person cried.

"Together!" another responded.

The Admiral grinned, and began chanting it loudly.

"We'll fix this!" he said. "Together! We'll fix this!"

Nearly every voice in the room was raised to join him in the next word, and The Admiral went on chanting until they had all jumped up from their seats. He moved across the space, walked through the sudden opening in the wall, and left the hooting assemblage behind.

Link felt his grip on the other man's reality begin to slip, and he held on tight to the vision as The Admiral stepped into the corridor. The last thing he saw was the woman who had helped him shut down Cervice openly waiting for him. She fell into step beside him, and began to speak in a fierce whisper.

"Did it work?" she said. "Are we separating?"

The Admiral resisted both smiling and nodding, for a moment. Even when he gave in, it was only to the nod.

"It worked," he said. "Humans and artificials will be directed to the appropriate ships, and we will have our opportunity."

She glanced over at him. The Admiral continued walking, staring straight ahead. Within his mind, Link redoubled his efforts to hold on another minute.

"What about families?" she said. "Many people have married them, or become similarly entangled; are they going to separate?"

The Admiral shrugged, continued his steady pace.

"They will," he said, "if they know what's good for them."

Link spiraled away from him, from the exchange and from the fleet somewhere deep in space. He landed in his body, sat up in bed, checked the time, and shook his head.

He took another pill.

TWENTY TWO

The mundane nature of his daily life had always bored Link. Knowing that everyone had to go through some kind of ritual just to stay alive had bothered him for as long as he could remember. No level of success existed that took away the need to move around at least a little, and feed yourself; the thought of someone else bathing him and brushing his teeth for him made Link more uncomfortable than the thought of doing it himself. Nonetheless, there was a level of discomfort that inherently went with life; through Link's eyes, the mundane was inextricably linked with that discomfort.

Watching helplessly from behind another man's eyes while he went through a routine meal and scrolled through what looked like some daily fleet newspaper on his log book screen, Link knew he should have been able to remain fascinated with even these small meaningless rituals. Subtle differences existed that had his mind reeling at first sight, and sighing with boredom in the next moment. The other man's mundane life was even more uninteresting than his own, and it was special torture in itself for Link to bear silent witness to it.

When The Admiral headed into a room that was smaller than any of the tiny spaces he had already seen, Link was immediately certain of the other man's intent. No matter the differences, alien technology seemed to resemble Earth's so far as the plumbing went. Link spent the next several minutes scratching at the edges of the consciousness he was inhabiting and wishing he had not taken another pill so soon. Even the thoughts in the other man's head were nothing but a garbled mess. As much as he had admired The Admiral for his ordered mind before, Link felt more at home in the nonsensical snippets he was hearing now.

The pill kept him locked in until The Admiral had finished his business, and washed his hands. Link wasn't sure if his efforts to vacate had jostled his consciousness loose, or if the pills were not working as well as they once had. It would certainly explain his inability to read the other man's thoughts as clearly as before. Waking up in his own skin was almost a perfunctory event at this point, and he began his wondering thought in one body and ended it in another. He sat up and sighed, mindlessly. With as little attention as he had put towards coming awake and sitting up, Link grasped the bottle of pills from the nightstand.

His only hesitation was that they were not working as well as before; Link considered taking two, thought better of it, and took a single pill. At this point he didn't need to wash it down; taking the pills had become second nature, and he'd had enough of mundane motions for the day. He lay down again, hoping against hope that there wasn't something even more disgusting coming. Longing for an actual torture session was not the right thing to do, so Link was careful not to do it.

The Admiral was with someone Link had never seen before, meeting in chambers that were both different and familiar in their own way. Link wondered if only high ranking people lived in such cramped quarters, in the fleet;

or if everyone was so short on space in space. The meeting was obviously clandestine, from where it was taking place; the other man did not keep his quarters as neat as The Admiral or Cervice, but Link didn't think those two were valid yardsticks of any measure.

Confidence was brimming over inside The Admiral, but otherwise Link couldn't tell just what was going on by looking out through his eyes. He could tell that the other man looked worried in nearly the same measure that The Admiral was feeling cocksure. Hoping he hadn't missed anything, Link was relieved and alarmed at the same time when the man spoke.

"You don't think Cervice is dead?" he asked.

The Admiral shook his head, and Link failed once again to dig deeply into his thoughts.

"I doubt it," The Admiral said. "He was a clever man, and an even more clever machine. If there was a way to back up his consciousness on file somewhere, he would have found it and done it."

The Admiral's companion coughed quietly, and smiled.

"Admiral," he said. "With all due respect, you clearly have no idea how consciousness transfer technology works."

From behind his eyes, Link watched The Admiral hold his usual stoic and humorless expression. Link may not have been able to hear his thoughts, but he could clearly feel the joy The Admiral was taking in watching the man's anxiety grip him once more. Now it was fear of The Admiral he was feeling, and The Admiral let him feel it until he could take it no longer. The man began to speak, to amend his statement; in the same moment, The Admiral cut him off.

"Of course, Mergo," he said. He did not smile. "Just as you have no idea how those things think, or feel. The only person who could have told us that turned on us after becoming one of them. It was you who discovered that Cervice was disrupting the electromagnetic field in the first place. You were the one who theorized that he may be attempting to take control of the fleet. Of all the people I should need to convince that decisive action must be taken, I never thought you would be the one downplaying this situation."

Link watched the fear growing in Mergo's eyes while he listened, and heard the desperation in his voice when he replied.

"I discovered that Cervice was disrupting the EMF," he said. "I never proposed that he was trying to take over the fleet, though; that was you, Admiral. I was unable to discover his intentions by simply studying his behavior. It's entirely possible that he was trying to fix it, and not telling the rest of us so as not to alarm us."

The Admiral nodded.

"Which is even worse," he scoffed, "as well as a clear indication of either his intentions or his delusions. It's one thing to know someone is nefarious, and out to hurt others. It's another thing entirely when that person has duped themselves into believing they are acting in the best interest of others. There is no end to the evil a self-righteous person can commit, in light of their own perceived greatness. If Cervice was willing to work on something as vital as the electromagnetic field generator without telling the rest of us, what lengths would he have gone to if we hadn't discovered his secrecy and prevented further meddling?"

In light of The Admiral's impassioned rant, the other man was either struck speechless or afraid to voice his feelings. He shrugged.

"Any or all of them could be working against us," The Admiral went on. "We are straddling a fence here, with our extinction on one side and theirs on the other. Tell me, old friend, that you would rather be remembered as a dead pacifist; and I'll leave you be. If you prefer to be the next Engineer, however…I could certainly use your help saving this fleet."

Mergo still looked uncertain. His gaze went out of focus for a moment, as he pictured some real or imagined perk he might enjoy should he be elevated to such an esteemed position. When his eyes found The Admiral's again, Mergo looked away immediately.

"Or half of it, anyway," he said, shifting uncomfortably.

Leaning in, The Admiral was delighted to see the other man draw away in fear.

"That's going to happen either way," The Admiral said. "We cannot decide whether or not half the fleet survives; all we can do is try and make sure it's the right half."

His voice went lower, and scorn dripped from every word.

"Can you imagine?" he sneered. "A fleet of robots drifting across the universe looking for a new home? At some point it would become their mission to destroy all organic life, if that isn't their intent already."

The other man shook his head.

"That's not possible," he said. "We programmed the very bedrock of their DNA to prevent them from hurting us. It's why they can't pilot the fleet; you know that."

The Admiral nodded adamantly, like the other man was making his point for him. He continued nodding as he spoke.

"It's also why they can't reproduce themselves," he said. "Because every generation has always been designed that way. By law."

He watched until Mergo inclined his head in assent before going on. The Admiral noted that the motion came after considerable hesitation, and Link noticed him taking note.

"Except now they can," The Admiral added.

Mergo shook his head adamantly, and opened his mouth to protest. The Admiral cut him off.

"While Cervice was in power," he said, "he quietly rescinded that ruling. Since there were only two leaders left, he had the ability to do so without consulting me. It's not just further evidence that he was working against us; it's essentially a declaration of war. I may have never discovered it if Cervice hadn't disappeared, and we could be headed to our own destruction by continuing to follow his lead."

Mergo's eyes had gone wide while he spoke, and now they darted back and forth in frantic patterns. He began wringing his hands, and beginning sentences that had no end.

"How did..." he began.

"Who knows..." he began again.

"How many..." he started, once more.

The Admiral was growing impatient, and cut him off.

"You're a senior programmer," he said. "How could this have happened? What are the possible repercussions?"

The panic was still gripping him, and Mergo's eyes continued to dart back and forth. Without a thought to warn Link, The Admiral struck the other man across the face. A resounding crack echoed off the tight metallic walls, and Mergo stepped back. He blinked twice, and frowned.

"Get ahold of yourself, man," The Admiral said. "If they knew about it, you would know about it. We can't afford the possibility that Cervice is alive, and telling them now."

Mergo had stopped looking at him like he was terrified The Admiral would hit him again. Now he was nodding, and staring off into the distance. A red mark had appeared on his cheek, after he had been struck; it had visibly faded, and was nearly gone. Link wondered, inside The Admiral's mind, if the chemical control bands had accelerated the healing. He made a mental note to ask Cervice about it.

"It's worse than that," Mergo said. "We designed the latest generation with a back door to bypass both restrictions. Cervice insisted on it, saying that the fleet could be broken up by any number of circumstances. If only artificials survived such an incident, or were separated from the rest of the fleet for some reason, he said they would need to be able to create others of their kind and defend themselves against hostile alien encounters. The back door doesn't only make their reproduction possible, though; it basically makes it a primal urge. They won't just be able to reproduce; they'll be compelled to. Once that back door is thrown open, they'll notice."

Mergo chuckled.

"Metaphorically, of course," he amended.

He sobered, mid-chuckle.

"But they will notice," he repeated. "It's inevitable."

Link had become accustomed to The Admiral's thoughts being a buzzing nonsensical wall of background noise. He had stopped trying to make sense of them long ago, and had decided the only real information he could get was from exchanges like these. Normally the other man was so calm inside, it was even more automatic for Link to ignore the way he was feeling as well. A sudden burst of anger took him by surprise as much as it did The Admiral. What the other man did next surprised him even more.

Looking down at the floor, The Admiral spoke quietly.

"You built this back door?" he said.

Mergo shrugged. Although his eyes were averted, Link

knew The Admiral saw it. They both felt the rage mounting, but there were no outward signs of his inner boil.

"We had to," Mergo said. "If The Engineer hadn't conceived of the consciousness transfer device, we would have been forced to use the back door just to get moving. We couldn't launch The Perpetual Dream without artificial intelligence guiding it, and any previous generation would have existed in a constant state of analysis paralysis looking for a path through space that endangered no one. Lucky for us, the consciousness transfer device worked."

When The Admiral's eyes left the floor, he made a concerted inner effort to drain the hate from them and fill them with understanding instead. He smiled, convincingly.

"Of course," he said. "Another device you designed, am I right?"

Mergo nodded, disarmed.

"Is it true," The Admiral pressed him, "that the device was built specifically to accommodate The Engineer's consciousness?"

After giving it a moment's thought, Mergo shook his head.

"It was designed with him in mind," he said. "But it wasn't made specifically for him. He thought we should say that, to prevent a drawn out debate over who should inhabit the central computer."

Mergo shrugged.

"But anyone could have used it," he said. "Theoretically."

Another tide of emotion swept through The Admiral's body, and Link felt his consciousness dislodged by the torrent. He grasped at the feeling helplessly as he spun away and into his own body.

He took another pill immediately.

At first Link thought it hadn't worked. He stared at the

inside of his eyelids so long that he grew bored, and tried to open them. With a lurch of fear, he tried to move.

Nothing happened.

The pill had worked. Link was in the other man's body, but the other man was sleeping. After only a minute he began to wonder if he was going to go quietly mad with boredom; in the next minute the dreams began, and Link spiraled helplessly into the nightmarish inner landscape of The Admiral's mind.

TWENTY THREE

Time had twisted and turned for him so many times, in so many ways, since Link had begun to visit the distant space colony. The last thing he had expected was to be awake in another man's dreams, but he should have known better. The hour had been getting late, as he journeyed into and back out of The Admiral's life; at some point, he was going to sleep. When he finally woke up from the disturbing experience, Link looked at the bottle of pills like it was the devil incarnate. He rolled over, closed his eyes and tried to sleep normally.

Sleep did come, but it was hardly normal. Those same nightmares haunted him, faceless and shapeless but terrifying in a way he had never known. Link was accustomed to his own ghosts; they were as ineffectual as he was, in his experience. These ghosts chased him with speed and haunted him with conviction; they were The Admiral's ghosts, and Link had no chance against them. Several times throughout the night he woke up sweating, his heart pounding in his chest. Long before his own planet's sun rose in the sky, his sheets were soaked and he was more tired from trying to sleep than he would be if he just woke up.

Link felt exhausted, drained, and at the end of his rope. He couldn't look his own eyes in the mirror as he brushed his teeth, and didn't like the feel of his own hands on his body while he showered. The fresh cup of coffee tasted of stale metal in his mouth, and the three bites of oatmeal he was able to coax down his throat felt like they were requiring far more energy to consume than they could possibly give him.

The sheets needed to be changed. He glanced at the bottle several times as he fitted the first sheet, and several more as he laid out the top sheet and the comforter. Each glance was followed quickly by a look at the clock on his nightstand.

He was going back. Link knew that, as surely as he knew he did not want to go back early. For nearly an hour, he sat on the freshly made bed. He didn't do anything, except sip at his coffee from time to time. After awhile, that got cold; Link sniffed at it, sipped it one last time, and set it aside. He yawned, glanced at the bottle and the clock, and shook his head.

Suddenly, Link stood.

"I'm such an idiot," he muttered. "I want him to be asleep. I need to take two pills, and talk to Cervice. I won't get caught in there again."

Speaking of the situation aloud had a strange effect on Link. His mind had started to unwind, and fog up with the desire for sleep; now he was alert, and decidedly awake. A thousand doubtful voices began to press at his mind, and demand that he look at what his life had turned into. From questioning the name of the robot that sent for him, to wondering what an electromagnetic field might have to do with memory, his thoughts were suddenly ablaze with wondering.

"It can't be real," he said. "This is all in my head."

Those words made him feel even better, and Link's panic had nearly completely subsided by the time he twisted open the bottle and took two pills. He woke almost immediately in The Admiral's body, and had a good look around.

Link shook his head.

"It sure looks real," he muttered.

The long steel corridors had become familiar terrain for him. Some folks were striding purposefully down the hallways, but not nearly as many as before. Link looked, when he could, and noted that everyone he saw had only one chemical control band in evidence. He found himself walking more quickly, trying not to panic inside. If all the artificials were gone, and Cervice was an artificial…

Finally, he came to the door that led into Cervice's cramped chambers. The door did not open at his approach, and Link didn't know any other way to activate it.

"Um, excuse me," he said. "Open this door."

For the next several silent moments, Link didn't know what to do. He looked up and down the hallway, cleared his throat and stepped toward the wall again.

The opening appeared suddenly, and he was standing face to face with a young woman he had never seen before. He glanced down, to see if she had lighted bands about her wrists; her hands were hidden, clasped behind her back.

"Can I help you, Admiral?" she said.

Link tried to look past her, to catch a glimpse of Cervice or someone else he might recognize. She leaned with him, blocking his view.

"Is…" Link began, then hesitated.

Biting his lip, he tried to see if her eyes were electric or organic.

Link shrugged.

"Is Cervice here?" he said.

Her eyes went wide, and he shook his head adamantly.

"I'm not the Admiral," he said. "I'm Link."

All the tension went out of her, in one dramatic sigh. She poked her head into the hallway, revealing her hands and the bands about her wrists as she did; then she ushered him inside, with a look of genuine irritation.

"You could've said something!" she said.

Link shrugged again.

"I thought you'd know," he said. "Sorry."

She faced him in the narrow gray hallway, and placed her hands on her hips.

"Sorry?" she said. "Do you know what is happening here? All artificials are being sent off the ship. They're giving us time, but not much. Cervice has been waiting for you. He's counting on you. We're all counting on you. They could come for him at any moment, and then where would we be? You're sorry? Don't be sorry! Help us!"

Link edged away from her as she spoke, until his back pressed against cold steel and he could retreat no further.

"Are you done?" he asked, when it seemed she was done.

She nodded.

"I'm here to help," he said. "Is Cervice in there?"

He pointed, to where the hallway ended.

She nodded again.

Turning her back, she moved toward the other door. She swept into the small space before him, and announced him with a wave of her hand.

"Our savior is here," she said. "I see why you're worried."

While Link shot her a look, Cervice stood from where he had been sitting. He looked like he was trying to suppress a laugh.

"Link," he said. "You have returned."

He got ahold of himself, and gave the woman an unappreciative glance as well.

"Thank you, Eria," he said. He glanced at the wall,

where the door had been a moment earlier.

After a pause, and an audible sigh, she left them alone together.

"I rode along," Link said. "I rode along in his mind, like you asked. I saw him convincing everyone to separate the fleet. He acted like it was what you would have wanted. He made it sound like you gave your life to save the fleet."

Cervice nodded thoughtfully. He motioned to one of the two chairs in the tight quarters, and sat in one while Link took the other.

"I might yet," he mused. "I might yet."

Link shifted uncomfortably, and Cervice laughed quietly.

"Is that all?" he said. "We already know we are being separated."

Leaning forward, Link shook his head.

"No," he said. "He spoke privately with someone, later. He says that he suspects you are still alive. He also suspects the robots of malicious intent. To him, the only way to survive is by getting rid of all of them."

Link thought on that, and decided to amend it.

"All of you," he said. "He wants to get rid of all of you."

Cervice said nothing, for so long that Link began to wonder quietly to himself. Soon he couldn't keep it quiet any longer.

"Did you mess with the EMF generator?" he said. "Was that why the memory issues began? And did you program artificials to—"

"Enough, Link," Cervice said, cutting him off. "We don't have much time. Once the other artificials have left the ship, they will scan for whoever is remaining. I can't hide from that, and I can't show my face. You've got to act decisively, Link; and you've got to do it now."

Link slid back into his seat, as far as it would allow. He crossed his arms in front of him, and frowned.

"What do you mean?" he said. "What do I need to do?"

The robot glanced down, and Link followed his electric eyes. When they fell on the weapon at his hip, they both looked up at the same time. Cervice fixed his gaze on him, and nodded.

"It's very simple to operate," he said. "Simply put it to your head, and pull the trigger. It will be over immediately, and you'll be back in your world and your own body. Maybe it would be better if you put it in your mouth, and aimed upward at the brain. You don't want to miss."

Link let his jaw drop open, and he stared incredulously at the robot.

"You want me to kill myself?" he whispered.

"Of course not," Cervice scoffed. "I want you to kill The Admiral. I want you to live a long life on your planet knowing that you saved my people. The only way you can do that now is by doing this. You must see that."

Holding his hand out before him, Link realized that he was trembling uncontrollably. He shook his head, trying to clear it, and only succeeded in disorienting himself further. Thoughts that were not his own began to race through his mind; Link gritted his teeth, and stood abruptly.

"He's coming back," he hissed. "I've got to get out of here."

Cervice stood as well, and ushered Link out into the hallway. He called out quietly, as Link stumbled away from him.

"Get as far away as you can," Cervice said.

Link glanced back, and saw that the door had closed. He moved along the wall as quickly as he could, leaning on it for support every few steps, until he lost complete control and catapulted back into his own body.

TWENTY FOUR

The most terrifying moments for him were the ones he spent helplessly staring out from behind The Admiral's eyes, wondering what horrible thing he would say or do next. Link could think of no other way to solve this situation, however; short of putting a gun in the other man's mouth, it was all he could come up with. He knew there was limited time, and great risk; but he also knew that he needed to exhaust all other possibilities before going for the most extreme option.

He went right from meeting with Cervice to popping a single pill and inhabiting The Admiral silently. The routines the other man went through suddenly took on a new meaning for Link. He watched The Admiral's thoughts as best he could, and found himself admiring how ordered and clear the mind he was inhabiting kept itself. Even the absent awareness that he gave his breathing and eating was of special interest to Link now; he watched the other man from the inside, alert for any line of thinking that might lead to a solution other than the one Cervice had proposed.

Another visit to the restroom was not as appalling as Link had found it before. Every activity The Admiral engaged in began to look like an opportunity to perform some ritual for the last time. No matter how mundane the task, Link could see some deeper meaning in the way the other man performed it that said something particular about him. Yet rather than soften his heart or give him pause, what he saw only strengthened his resolve. This man was mad, in a way that would hurt others if he could.

When he woke up, Link swallowed another pill immediately and took up his watchful post once more. Every moment he looked out from those eyes only served to convince him completely that he had to do what Cervice had asked of him. The man spoke to others as if they weren't human, even when they were. He presumed only he could lead all of those people, and that he should not have to consult anyone in making his decisions.

Link's doubts had arisen around some of the things The Admiral had said about Cervice. Now he realized that it was surely projection; The Admiral had become all the things he had been accusing the robot of being all along. No evidence existed of Cervice's supposedly nefarious intentions; with every meeting The Admiral had, every word he spoke or thought, the evidence against him mounted in Link's mind.

The next time he woke up, The Admiral was just getting to his chambers. The young woman he had been colluding with from the beginning was there, waiting. She stepped up to him and threw her arms around him, right there in the hallway. Link had seen no more telling indication that they felt victory was already theirs, the way they held each other openly and laughed. Link let the thread go, to give the other man another last moment in privacy.

In his own body, Link went to the bathroom and went through his own mundane routine. A quick glance in the mirror surprised him; there was less stubble on his face than he had expected, and he had apparently lost a few pounds. He brushed his teeth and showered, made himself a cup of coffee and scrambled two eggs. It was all like the toothpaste, dull and chalky and flavorless. Link left the unfinished cup and half the eggs on the end table in the living room, abandoning the comfort of his easy chair for the mussed familiarity of his bed.

Half of his mind was bent on not thinking about what he had to do, while the other half was intent on steeling him for the event; it left nothing for bodily sensations like flavor or comfort. Link lowered himself to the mattress in his pajamas and let his internal battle rage on for a few more minutes. The Admiral should be going to sleep soon, and Link was determined to make sure the other man never woke up again.

He took two pills, swallowed them dry and lay down once more. The pounding thrum of his heartbeat kept him awake for several minutes, but eventually the spinning sensation started. Link let himself be washed away by it, hoping with all he was that this would be the last time.

The Admiral's chambers were dark, and the woman was gone. Link sat up in the other man's bunk, and looked around for the pistol. His eyes fell on a half dozen things he had seen many times and never asked about; he mused sadly that he would never know. Once he found the weapon, Link went to The Admiral's desk and sat down. The log was there, laid out flat and as devoid of new entries as every other time he had looked at it lately. Link considered writing some kind of suicide note, but thought better of it and shook his head.

He had one last good look around, the memories of the experiences he'd had on this ship washing over him. Tears filled The Admiral's eyes, and Link let them fall down the other man's face.

Opening his mouth, Link put the barrel between his teeth.

He closed his eyes, and more tears leaked out. Link squeezed the trigger, or tried to; the command wasn't obeyed, and he opened his eyes to look at the offending digit.

"No."

Link whirled, and the gun went clattering to the floor. Of course he was alone; there had been no voice behind him. He picked up the pistol once more, and moved it toward his face.

"NO!"

He dropped the weapon, but this time it wasn't him dropping it. That voice had not been behind him; it had been inside his head. Inside The Admiral's head. Link waited, listening. When he realized there was nothing but silence to listen to, he let out a heavy sigh. In the time he had remaining, he went to find Cervice.

The robot was not pleased to see him.

"Why is he still alive?" Cervice demanded.

Link spread his hands.

"I tried," he said. "Some primal instinct took over. He stopped me."

The robot sat up straight, his eyes going wide.

"He stopped you?" he said.

"No, not him." Link shook his head. "Some unconscious part of him. So far as I can tell, he has no idea what we are trying to do."

Cervice collapsed back into his chair, dejected.

"It doesn't matter either way," he said. "If you can't take him out, we are powerless to prevent his plan."

Link frowned, and stomped his foot.

"I refuse to accept that," he said. "I know I can still do something. At the very least, I can keep him out of his own body as much as possible. How much harm can he do if I just keep taking the pills?"

The robot perked up a little.

"You may as well try," Cervice said. "We've got some time. Apparently many of the service droids on the ship utilize a type of artificial intelligence that helps them learn and avoid repeating mistakes. They are teaching the computer to distinguish between these and the sentient artificials, but it is not going to be easy."

Link felt his eyes light up, and he snapped The Admiral's fingers.

"I'll give orders," he said. "I'll tell everyone that I changed my mind, and that we need to stop separating and try to recover you electronically. You can just show up, and take control again."

Cervice laughed, bitterly.

"I was never in control," he said. "I was the bridge between a people and its creation, which had surpassed them. I was the only way for both people and artificials to work together, to live together, and to find a new home together. The only way the fleet can act as one is if I am directing that interface. I would need undisturbed access to the central computer for some time to reengineer the interface. At some point you would have to relinquish The Admiral's body to him, even if only for a few minutes. He would act quickly, and decisively."

Throwing up his hands, Link cried out.

"Can't you just kill me?" he exploded.

The robot shook his head.

"Of course not," he said. "Artificials can't harm humans."

Link paced the small space even less effectively than he could his living room.

"What about the back door?" he said. "Isn't there a back door?"

After a moment's confusion, Cervice shook his head again.

"The back door for what?" he said. "For artificial propagation? Are you aware that we can't reproduce ourselves? Without humans, artificials would inevitably die out. The only things we can't do is reproduce or hurt people, and those are abilities we need to live on as a race. Unfortunately, the back door does not actually become viable until decades after one of us has seen a living human. That's why it's a back door; it is to be activated only in the worst conditions. It has been activated, but it will not come online in time for us to do anything. Even this body I inhabit required that a human be part of its creation."

Link did his best to ignore the robot's dejected tone and body language. He crossed his arms resolutely, and gave Cervice a steely stare.

"I can still help," he said. "I'm sure of it."

The robot waved an artificial hand

"Do what you will, Link," he said. "It can't get much worse."

TWENTY FIVE

Link let The Admiral get his sleep, while he tossed and turned in his own bed. The rest was not refreshing, like it had been before; any connection between sleep and renewal he'd had seemed like it had been severed by his new connection to another world. Link was convinced that would change, once he fulfilled the purpose Cervice had spoken of. His only good reason for sleeping without taking any pills was that The Admiral was in a sleep cycle himself. They may as well both get their rest, even if it did neither of them any good.

The nightmare landscape of the other man's mind while he slept still haunted Link. Taking a single pill and witnessing that twisted carnival of thoughts and feelings and images was the last thing he wanted to consider. Even in his waking moments, in his own life, he felt the knuckles of The Admiral's mind dragging through the soupy morass of his own thoughts. He had learned all he needed to with one night in that hell, and there was little he wouldn't do to keep from returning.

If he took two pills, he may be in control again; but what good could he do? Without the ability to literally pull the trigger, Link would be completely in charge and totally helpless all at the same time.

As the night wore on, Link spent more time waking up and wondering than he did actually sleeping. He racked his brain whenever it was not dozing or spinning helplessly, and gave up finally when the first rays of sunlight squeezed through the narrow cracks in the bedroom blinds. Getting up, he brushed his teeth and showered with almost zero attention on the tasks as he performed them. In the refrigerator, he reached past the eggs to seize the creamer. Coffee sounded better than food, and even that precious brew tasted of a habit long since broken. After only half the cup was gone, Link poured the rest out and padded into his bedroom once more.

He still wasn't certain what he was going to do, but Link knew he had to do something. Shaking two of the pills out of the bottle and into his hand, he tossed them into his mouth together. He swallowed, nodded resolutely and tossed back the comforter and top sheet. Part of him couldn't believe how badly he wanted to drift off again, while another part of him wondered why he would want to do anything other than sleep. The tug of war didn't last long, however; soon Link felt his mind moving through space, and into the other man's body.

The Admiral had clearly been awake for awhile, and Link delighted in having missed both his morning walk and breakfast. He went immediately to the other man's chambers, and rushed to the log where it was sprawled open on the desktop. Surely he had caught up by now, and Link could figure out what to do next based on what he had written.

He slowed as he approached the slim sheet, and saw that there was indeed a new entry. Two lines stood out on the page, written in big block letters that called out to him from several feet away. Link stopped short, and read the simple sentences.

I KNOW WHO YOU ARE, LINK.
YOU HAVE ALREADY LOST.

As soon as he read his own name in the other man's hand, Link felt his heart begin to pound. He pivoted in place and bolted for the door, nearly colliding with the metal as it slid away to create the opening. Every corridor seemed ten times longer than it had before, and he raced desperately down each of them with no concern for the few curious onlookers he passed. At last he came to the hallway that would take him to Cervice, and sprinted around the corner. Link saw the outpost right away, and slowed his steps.

Two men stood bracketing the entrance, facing forward. They both turned as he bounded up the hallway, and gave him a respectful nod. Link continued toward them at a measured pace, trying to hide his panic. As he got close, he called out to them.

"You boys look hungry," he said. "Stand down, and go get something to eat. I'll take the situation from here."

He finished speaking as he neared them, and walked as though he expected them to move further apart. Instead they crowded together, and blocked his way. They exchanged a look of uncertainty, but held their ground. After a pause, and another doubtful glance, one of them spoke.

"Admiral," he said. "As per your orders, I must ask you a question."

Link felt like a balloon that had sprung a sudden leak. He tried to keep his shoulders straight, and feign impatience.

"Out of my way," he said. "I've got to get in that room."

The sentries shifted, and looked at each other once more; neither of them moved, except to come a little closer together.

"Admiral," the sentry repeated. "As per your orders—"

"Ask me," Link snapped, cutting him off. "Stop wasting my time."

For a moment Link thought they were going to respond to that, and put some space between them. Both men were clearly uncomfortable with deliberately standing in his way. Then they looked at each other again, and the sentry that had remained silent spoke.

"Sir," he said. "Where is Cervice?"

Link made every effort he could to comb The Admiral's mind for the answer they expected. A strange kind of silence answered his search, even more distant and empty than the senseless mumble he had grown accustomed to. He looked at the door, wishing it would open, and heard his heart pounding frantically in his chest.

"He's dead," Link blurted, finally. "Cervice is dead."

Without warning, one of the men leapt forward and seized his arm. The other held back, confusion twisting his face, and Link tore free while he hesitated. He dashed up the hallway, reaching for the pistol at his side as he ran. Footsteps thudded on the steel floor behind him, and both men began shouting. Link kept running, the gun in his hand, and didn't look back.

They were both faster than him. The first one tackled him easily, and knocked the gun from his grasp. The second piled on before they hit the floor together, and Link found himself suddenly at the bottom of a heavy and suffocating heap. His arms were yanked painfully behind him, and his hands were bound before he could get his bearings. One of the men stood up and yanked him painfully to his feet, while the other regained his own footing. They marched him back towards the door he had been trying to get through, speaking as if he was no longer there.

"It's true, then," one man said. "The Admiral was right."

Link could see the other man nod from the corner of his eye.

"I guess so," he said. "There's no way this is him. The Admiral would never go down so easy, or do such an awful job defending himself."

Pulling at them as they led him through the first door, Link felt them move with him. He tried to shove his way into one of them, and got yanked off balance to smash painfully into the other.

"That's ridiculous," he said, desperately. "Do you hear what you're saying? Look at me. I'm The Admiral."

They each glanced at him, then at each other. One of them laughed. They halted before the doorway that had led him to Cervice before, just short of triggering it to open.

"Whoever you are," one said. "You will be held here until you can prove you are who you say you are. It's clear that you aren't, right now."

The other stepped forward, and an opening appeared in the wall. Beyond the doorway the room was vacant. Link could tell that they were watching him closely, and he tried not to react in any way to the empty room. He let them coax him inside, and the door slid into place behind him.

Link looked around, trying not to give away what he was looking for to any electronic eyes. He found nothing, no evidence to either suggest that Cervice had been discovered or had gotten away. Every now and then he shouted a vague answer to their question, assuming someone could hear.

"Cervice is with all of us!" he tried first, remembering what The Admiral had said in the assemblage earlier. After half a minute passed with no response, he tried again.

"Cervice is in our legends," he said, feeling pathetic.

The answer could well be that he was on the run, or back in a body that looked just like he did as The Engineer.

Link couldn't take that risk, though; if they didn't know where or who he was, telling them would both give them information they didn't have and still be the wrong response. He would be locked up, while they were free to go about searching with renewed vigor and further insight.

Link frittered away the moments he had in the other man's body, hoping against all hope that the answer to the question was not that Cervice was locked up and being tortured somewhere. He wondered if the robot could shut off the pain, or if he would have to endure it like anyone else. Every time he thought of a possible response that was vague enough to shout out, he did so.

No reply ever came.

TWENTY SIX

At last, Link woke again in his own body. He thought of taking another single pill immediately, to jump back into The Admiral's mind as an observer; if he was quick enough, he might hear the answer they were looking for and be able to use it later. Experience told him it would not be so easy; missing the moment would make it a worthless trip, and he would be locked in as a helpless bystander until the pill wore off.

His phone was on the nightstand. Link seized it and pressed the home button, wondering first what day it was and second what hour. Nothing happened, and he realized the battery had died sometime in the last however many days of solid useless sleep he had gotten. One question could be answered by glancing at the alarm clock. Padding into the living room, he plugged the device in and let it be. The other answer had to wait until his phone had charged a few minutes. Link made himself a cup of coffee while he waited, and sipped at it mechanically.

The warm brew tasted even more off, somehow. Link was sure it was the fact that he wasn't eating much, although he still had no desire to rustle up a few bites to go with the sweetened caffeine. After a few more sips he went to check the expiration date on the creamer. If anything, the number of weeks before a dairy based product was set to be tossed should have been alarming: it was nowhere near expiring.

Link tilted a little more of the sugary stuff into his mug, and put the container back in the refrigerator. Sipping at it as he moved, ignoring the metallic aftertaste, he made his way to the living room to check his phone. He sighed, relieved at the date. Although it was the first day of the year today, he had the next day off to celebrate the holiday. Ordinarily he would have thought it was a great way to start a new year, having the first Monday off paid. Now he took it as a sign, telling him he had a purpose to fulfill and giving him one more chance to do it.

Yawning, Link slurped the remainder of his coffee and headed for the bedroom once more. He couldn't believe how tired he felt, but he supposed it was for the best. The most important thing he had to do awaited on the other side of sleep, after all. He took two pills, and lay down in his pajamas.

The Admiral was on his way somewhere. At first it seemed right there in his thoughts, and Link reached out mentally to snare it. Like a drifting dream, it slipped away; and Link was left alone in another's quiet mind. He tried to let his feet move on their own, and perhaps follow the path they had been programmed by his subconscious to take. Instead he stood there motionless in the hallway, with no motivation but his own.

He dared not stand around too long, or act out of sorts in a public area. If any of The Admiral's people challenged him, Link would end up spending more time locked away and unable to act at all. He had to think, and figure out where Cervice would be if he was still alive. As soon as he moved past a junction in the corridors he grew increasingly uneasy. Link knew he may be drawing suspicion by not heading one way or another to some appointed meeting. He hadn't made it a dozen steps before he stopped again, and turned in his tracks.

They had only ever met in a handful of places. The Admiral's quarters were out of the question, as was the cramped similar space Cervice had occupied for a short period. Cervice didn't even know Link had seen them interacting in the command center, and that wasn't a likely place to hide anyhow. Only one place stood out in his memory, and Link headed there without hesitation. He prided himself on his purposeful stride, and making no outward sign of his internal alarm. Every person he passed wore only one chemical control band, and openly displayed their bare limbs. Link was either looking for the last artificial on the ship or for something that was not there at all.

Stepping into the cafeteria, Link was glad to find it deserted. He poked his head into the hallway, made sure the coast was clear, and stepped back inside. He called out quietly.

"Cervice," he said. "Are you here?"

Nothing happened.

"It's Link," he added, hopefully.

He remembered then that The Admiral knew his name somehow. What if he had tried this same trick, and lured Cervice out with it?

Link felt his heart begin pounding at the thought, and he turned in a slow circle with his hands over his face. Shaking his head, he dislodged the thought and had another.

"Did The Admiral try this already?" he said. "Did he fail because you're gone or because he didn't have enough information?"

After stepping one foot into the corridor once more, and having a good look in both directions, Link went on.

"I don't care about your people," he said. "I mean, your history and stuff. I care about saving you, but I hate it when you drone on about where you all come from."

Link chuckled.

"Get it?" he said. "Drone?"

No reply was forthcoming, as he turned another slow circle.

"You think I'm totally inept," he sighed, finally. "You have shown very little confidence in me helping you effectively from the moment we met."

A panel disappeared in the wall, and a service robot trundled out. It got close, and he knelt to its height as it neared.

"Link?" The voice was flat and artificial, but relieved.

Link nodded enthusiastically, and found himself fighting back tears. He wanted to hug the contraption, but couldn't see a way to comfortably put his arms around it. Instead he stood up, stepped back and looked down at it.

"I'm so glad you made it," Link whispered.

Two appendages sprouted mechanically from the robot's sides, and gestured vaguely at the rest of it.

"This is hardly what I would consider making it," it said.

Link beamed, despite himself.

"At least you're alive," he said. "In some form. Do you have any ideas? What can we do?"

The robot was still, after retracting its appendages once more. Link remembered how nice it had been to be able to read Cervice's expressions, even if only for a little while.

"Right now," it said, finally, "is not a good time. We would look suspicious together, and the last thing you need to do is arouse suspicion."

Link shifted uncomfortably from one foot to the other. "Um…" he said. "About that…"

The robot rolled backward a bit and then forward again, the only emotional reaction it could muster.

"Have you been discovered?" it demanded.

Link nodded.

"I spent my last tour of duty in custody," he said.

A whirring sound emitted from the housing of the metal device, as if Cervice was trying to sigh with inadequate audio options.

"I suspected as much. That means right now is definitely not the time," it said. "Unless you are prepared to shoot anyone we see on the way."

Reaching down to lightly finger the pistol The Admiral always wore on his hip, Link pulled his hand away like it was hot to the touch.

"I don't know if I can…" he began. "On the way where?"

"I've got to try to get back in," Cervice said. "You need to take me to the main interface, and help me download back into it."

Link felt his eyes go wide, and he waved his hands a little frantically.

"They will be guarding that, don't you think?" he bristled. "And how do you even know it will work? What if they locked you out permanently? Or set a trap for you? Didn't you say that would take awhile? How can I hold on that long?"

The robot waited patiently, until he was done.

"This is our last chance, Link," it said. "There is no more being careful, or biding our time. I have stayed out of his reach as long as I can. Surely The Admiral has separated the fleet by now, and is preparing to annihilate the artificials and anyone that has chosen to stand beside them. We must act, tonight."

Link fidgeted uselessly.

"What if it doesn't work?" he repeated.

The robot didn't hesitate.

"We shut it down," it said. "We shut it down and reboot, and hope for the best when everything comes back online."

Stepping back, Link shook his head.

"Doesn't that shut down everything?" he said. "And everyone?"

"It does," the robot responded. "It also puts all of our navigation, weapons and service systems on automatic. Everyone lives, but no one remembers who they used to be."

Link was still shaking his head, incredulous.

"Even you," he pointed out. "Right?"

"Even me," Cervice said. "A sacrifice I am willing to make, if it ensures the survival of so many people."

Sighing heavily, Link stepped forward and knelt down again.

"Wait," he said. "Just give me a little time. Let me ride along and watch again, and find out what he knows and exactly what he is doing. There has to be a way to stop him that doesn't involve me finding out if I have it in me to kill people."

The contraption slid silently away from him, toward the panel that disappeared as it approached. It called back to him as it moved.

"That's your concern," it said. "A question you must answer for yourself. If you do answer it, and find that you still want to help, you will see that I am correct. Then it becomes a matter of using the weapon skillfully, something I am not certain you can do. In any case, be quick. We may already be too late."

It stopped, before going through the opening.

"You know I must serve him food," it said. "I clear his dirty dishes when he is done. I wonder the whole time if he has found me out, and is here to destroy me before he moves on to the next course."

Link knew the robot couldn't reproduce the subtle tones that a human or artificial throat could. Still, he couldn't help but wonder how it felt inside that awkward metal box as the panel slid back into place without a sound. Cervice seemed more confident in his own demise than he was in Link's ability to help.

He was not so sure the robot was wrong.

TWENTY SEVEN

For the first time in a good long while, Link slept soundly through the night. He woke feeling as refreshed as he could hope to, and even made a little bowl of oatmeal to go with his coffee. Although he'd had a good night's sleep, Link began to feel tired almost immediately. He knew one good sleep was not enough to get caught up, so it didn't worry him. After the oatmeal had settled, and the coffee was gone, he took a single pill and crawled between the sheets.

Link had never really troubled himself with wondering about things like God, or whether some kind of higher power existed. He felt insignificant enough around other people; it was hard for him to imagine a person or power so important paying him any special notice. If there was something out there, surely she or he or it had better things to worry about than whether or not someone who would rather literally do nothing ever again believed deeply in it or him or her.

Now, he had to wonder. Either Cervice was right, and some kind of mathematical justice existed in the universe after all; or he was way more lucky in this world than he was in his own.

The Admiral was somewhere Link had never seen, but it only took a moment of watching from behind the other man's eyes before he figured it out. Together, they faced a wall that looked more formidable than the other metal walls on the ship somehow. The Admiral was holding his pistol before him, aiming at the only thing that stood between them and the wall. Another piece of dark metal, it was shaped like a figure and affixed to the floor.

When The Admiral squeezed off a round, it did not surprise him any more than it did the other man. He was right at the edges of his own consciousness, open and deliberate with his thoughts. The piece of metal that disappeared would have been the figure's left eye, if it had one. Instead a perfect round hole appeared, smoked slightly for the space of a slow breath, and promptly disappeared. Like the doorways, metal swam and shifted and reformed seamlessly.

The Admiral pulled the trigger again.

Once more, a hole formed suddenly in the lifeless hunk of metal. This one was dead center, and would have been a shot right between the eyes. The Admiral nodded quietly to himself, and made another hole in the same spot as soon as the figure reformed. Link listened carefully to the other man's thoughts, and paid special attention to the way he held the weapon and where he put his eyes. The next twenty minutes or so were like an advanced lesson in marksmanship, and Link felt confident he was learning a great deal more than he could have spending all day with the pistol and the target and his own inexperienced mind.

The next place The Admiral went reminded Link that his luck was not always so good, and the other man shut his mind down once more as he sat in the private space and did his natural space business. It gave Link the opportunity to think maybe there was more truth in the East, and their way of seeing things. Perhaps for every great good to exist, there must be a great evil to balance it. Or at least something really disgusting.

Link didn't notice the lack of energy in The Admiral's steps until he made it where he was headed next, and approached a man in a very similar uniform.

"Admiral, sir," the man said, standing to attention.

Slowing his steps, The Admiral spoke gruffly.

"Dark Star Pilot," he said. "Carry on."

The Admiral shifted, and began to move past him.

"Sir," the pilot said, stepping in front of him. "I'm sorry, but—"

"Cervice is in our midst," The Admiral spat. "I believe that is the one for today. Or you could try to fight me. Rumor has it the imposter can't handle himself, and I'm down for a quick tumble."

The pilot stepped aside.

"Of course, sir," he said. "Carry on. You just...look different today. Maybe you're tired. Have you been getting your rest?"

The Admiral shook his head.

"I can't trust myself to go to sleep," he muttered. "It's only for another day or two. In the meantime, I'm taking sleep pills to stay sharp. As soon as our enemy no longer threatens our lives, I will get caught up on my rest. I appreciate your concern. Status update."

The man straightened abruptly, and walked away from him. The Admiral followed, and soon they stood before the screen Link had seen on his first visit to the ship. Where a starry landscape had stretched to infinity before, the area was so cluttered with ships that Link could count the number of distant suns still visible on one hand. He reeled inside the other man's mind as he tried to tally the spaceships.

From the size of a travel trailer camper to what he could only describe as a small planet, the number of vessels in sight was not in the hundreds. It may not have been in the thousands, even. Link stopped trying to count, or group them in rough estimates he might add together, and let his mind simply boggle for a long shocked moment. He wondered how many people each ship could hold, and how many of them would be nothing but space dust soon if he did nothing to stop it.

Some of them were distinctive in their design, and looked almost nothing like the others. Most of the ships were the same basic layout, however; as if one mind had engineered a model, and scaled the others in size while duplicating every outer aspect of it endlessly. A central globe was the bulk of the design, and all of them rotated at what appeared to be varying speeds; it was hard to tell, with the size differences and the sheer number of crafts in the small amount of space. Each globe was spinning on the axis created by the other part of the craft. Curved and slim, metal arms reached around the sphere to embrace it at opposite ends. Where the arms came together, small to giant engines jutted out behind it to propel the entire mechanism through space.

The common design meant nothing to Link, but the sheer number of ships was overwhelming. Each of them glowed with their own diffused light, and the overall effect was astounding. Like a city in full dark, the ships made their own skyscape with no ground to attach to and no moon to compete with. A full minute passed before he realized a conversation was happening, and that he should be listening to what was being said. Link tried to ignore the awesome sight on the giant screen, and tune into the exchange.

"...have been helping without knowing," the pilot was saying. "In putting themselves between us and the asteroid field, they have grouped together to make attacking them even easier."

The Admiral snorted his contempt.

"They're still mining," he said. "And hoarding resources. They are preparing to survive without us, building up their stores."

Glancing over his shoulder at the spectacle, the other man shrugged.

"They say they are protecting us," he pointed out. "That the mining is for all of us to share when we reunite."

Shaking his head, The Admiral pointed.

"They have positioned outliers," he said. "They are ready to take off in every direction, without hesitating or shifting at all. The rest of them are all pointed away from us, toward the mining operations. If they get any distance into the asteroid field without damage, we'll lose track of them almost immediately. Do you not see that they are clearly planning to either attack us or abandon us, or both?"

A look of genuine concern came over the pilot's face.

"That would be suicide," he protested. "Even if they can reproduce their own kind now, they can't attack us. We made them."

The Admiral gave him a look of genuine disappointment, and moved closer to the screen. He indicated clusters of ships with his hand as he spoke once more.

"Look at them," he said. "And this group here. Put yourself in their position, and think of the big picture. Imagine you want to destroy us. What would you do? How would you lay out your ships?"

He looked from The Admiral to the giant screen, so many times and so swiftly that he appeared to be shaking his head. At last, his eyes came to rest on The Admiral's.

"I would do just what they have," he murmured.

His eyes went wide, and he looked out at the ships once more. The Admiral stood next to him, watching him for a reaction. When it didn't come swiftly enough, he pressed the pilot further.

"You remember the first artificial intelligence," The Admiral said. "You remember how childlike they were, how hard it was for them to learn and how long they took to assimilate the simplest lesson. That was less than a dozen cycles ago. Back then, we thought they would never be our equals, in any way. We thought their numbers would be restricted naturally by their limited use and how much time and material went into building just one of them."

The other man was nodding, watching the same scene that had awed Link only minutes earlier. A frown creased his face, and his eyes had narrowed to angry slits.

"Not long ago," The Admiral went on, "we were all shocked to find that they could now reproduce themselves. That goes against all that we know of them, or so it seems. Yet if you think back, no contradiction exists. Every thing we once expected them to never be able to do, they can now do. The least of them is equal or superior to the greatest of us, in virtually every way. Their ability to reproduce is not a surprise, if you look at the progression of the artificial through time. It's expected."

Trembling slightly, the pilot turned to him once more.

"If you think of it that way," he breathed, "them attacking us..."

He trailed off, and The Admiral finished his thought for him.

"Is inevitable," he said. "Not a matter of if, but when."

TWENTY EIGHT

Link didn't have to take another pill to learn what The Admiral was doing. He clung to the other man's consciousness as long as he could, watching him have conversations with several people that were much like the exchange he'd had with the pilot and Mergo earlier. Somehow he had a knack for making others see things his way, and one questioning mind after another was soon swimming in the swirling sea of his answers. Even Link had to wonder, considering The Admiral's experience and determination, if there was maybe a shred of truth behind his fears. Every person he spoke with seemed as smart or smarter than Link, and they each walked away convinced.

When he woke up, Link felt a lot better about the whole situation. The Admiral was clearly taking his time speaking with each person that would be key to the attack. As angry as most of them became, at his gentle urging, he assured them that it was best to bide their time. The more hours that passed with no sign of their intent, the more likely they were to lull the artificial enemy into a false sense of security.

He couldn't see what The Admiral was thinking, but Link suspected he was still harboring some hope of finding Cervice and imprisoning or destroying the robot. The passphrase he had used may have been meaningless, but it didn't seem that way. If The Admiral thought Cervice was on one of those ships cluttering up this section of space, Link was sure the attack would have been well underway by now.

After waiting until nearly his own bedtime, Link took two pills and set his alarm for the morning. As soon as he woke in The Admiral's body, he dressed in the other man's uniform and strapped on his pistol. He had to play the same game, to draw Cervice out.

"It's me, Cervice," he called quietly. "It's Link. As you'll recall, I'm a huge disappointment. I do silly and stupid stuff. Like this."

Link did a soft-shoe, there in the deserted cafeteria. A panel opened in the wall, and the robot was already talking before the wall had reformed behind it.

"Finally, Link," it said. "Are you ready to help me?"

Link shook his head, and smiled when the whirring started.

"No," he said. "There's something I have to do first."

The robot couldn't take a deep breath, without lungs. It seemed to do something similar, as if winding up to barrage him with words.

"We don't have time," it said. "We have to—"

"Why didn't you tell me?" Link demanded, cutting it off.

Trundling back and then forward, Cervice stopped in the same place.

"Tell you what?"

Link shrugged, looked around the empty space.

"How many of them there are," he said. "I saw the ships. There are so many. Like, thousands. Tens of thousands."

Cervice was silent long enough to make him wonder what sort of thoughts were racing through the robot's mind.

"That is only half the fleet," Cervice reminded him. "And you are still underestimating. Our planet was much larger than yours, remember. We did not experience a population problem until there were tens of billions of us. When the artificials became easier to produce, our population nearly doubled over a short period of time. We were already in space, before our planet became imperiled. It was just a matter of getting the rest of us into space as well."

The robot fell silent, then spoke again.

"Or most of us, anyway," he said.

Placing his hands on his hips, Link stared down at the robot.

"You could have told me," he said. "You should have told me. I thought there were a few hundred people depending on me. Maybe a few thousand. But billions?"

It remained impossible to tell what Cervice was thinking while the robot sat there unresponsive. By the tone of its voice when it did speak, Cervice was wishing the metal housing had a head it could shake.

"What does it matter?" Cervice said. "When you know one person will be responsible for killing hundreds, how does the urgency of the situation increase when you add some zeroes on the end? How can morality be swayed by numbers? How is two different than two billion?"

Link had no answer for him. He shrugged, and turned to walk away.

Cervice called out after him.

"Where are you going?" the robot demanded. "Will you not do the right thing unless you are praised and coddled, no matter how many lives are at stake?"

Laughing quietly, Link ducked his head into the corridor. When he saw that it was vacant, he moved back into the cafeteria.

"I am going to help you," he said. "First, I need to do something. The Admiral won't move until he finds you, I'm sure of it. He wants you to watch him win, I think. So don't get found."

He left the robot with its questions and its sour mood. Now that he knew where the pistol range was, he could put the time he had to good use and get familiar with the weapon when he had control of the other man's hands. Link was glad to find the area empty. When the first few shots went wildly off target, he was even more grateful to be alone. The wall behind the target took the blasts silently, without judgement, and reformed into perfect wall again after each shot.

Remembering the lessons The Admiral had repeated in his head, Link took careful aim with the next shot. He breathed normally, squeezing the trigger on the exhale. Somehow the searing ray took off the target's shoulder, instead of the head he had been aiming at; but it was still gratifying to hit something other than the wall.

Link kept at it for as long as he could, until he felt the other man's mind begin to claw at the edges of his consciousness. He hurried to The Admiral's chambers, stripped the body to its underclothes, and crawled into his bunk.

TWENTY NINE

Link couldn't remember the last time he had headed to work feeling happy about going there. He'd never had a real and true enemy, or fought a battle that meant anything to anyone but him. As easy as his job was for him, he was seeing it in a whole new light after the time away. He was actually looking forward to discharging his daily duties, and earning his place in his own world. Later on, he was going to save another one.

The new year felt like a fresh start, and he was determined to get every aspect of his life on track. He even enthusiastically greeted a couple people as he passed them on the way to his cubicle. They looked at him a little strangely, but that was to be expected; they would get used to the new and improved Link by the end of the week.

Settling in at his desk, Link got right to work. He made sure to imbed some mistakes, since there were as many hours in new Link's day as there had been in old Link's day; he knew he would have plenty of time to go back later and fix them, even if he helped out a half dozen people throughout the day. When the first batch was finished he stood up, stretched, and had a slow stroll through the office.

Generally he didn't pay any attention to the nameplates affixed to the outer wall of each cubicle; today, he made it a point to notice each one he passed. After walking by one with a familiar name on it, he stopped and backed up to the entrance.

"Knock, knock," he said, poking his head in.

Steve swiveled in his chair, and gave him a pained smile.

"Oh," he said. "Hey, Link."

Link behaved as though he had been invited in, moving his whole body into the cramped space as he looked around. Only a few pictures adorned the short walls, and they were all of the same person.

"Look at this," Link said. "You already decorated. Who's in all the pictures? Your little sister? Your niece?"

The smile on his face had fallen, and only a pained expression remained. Steve sighed, and shook his head.

"That's my daughter," he said.

Link's eyebrows shot up, and he leaned in to inspect the closest photo.

"She's pretty adorable," he said. "I didn't know you had a kid."

Steve shrugged.

"You never asked," he said, simply.

His eyes went to the image Link was looking at, and he nodded.

"She is pretty adorable," he added. "Thanks."

Turning halfway in his chair, toward the computer, Steve let his gaze drift back to his work.

"I appreciate you training me, and all," he said. "But, uh, I really need to get back to work."

Link was still leaning in, his eyes on the photo. He straightened, glanced sideways at Steve and nodded.

"Alright, then," he said, awkwardly.

By the time he made it to the break room, Link had shaken off the exchange. Steve was likely just concerned about people thinking he was still not able to work without Link's help, and he got that. Not everyone could make the job look as easy as Link did. He got a cup of coffee, creamed it up, and headed confidently up the hallway. The door to Sherry's office was open, and he leaned casually into the jamb until she looked up from her computer.

"Hi Sherry," he said, straightening.

She stared at him for what felt like an eternity. Sherry's eyes spoke of layers of hurt and anger, and a familiarity he could not account for.

"Hi Sherry?" she echoed. "Really, Link? Oh, that's rich."

One moment she was looking at him in a way that made Link feel very uncomfortable; the next she turned her attention back to the lighted screen he couldn't see. As he listened to her fingers start clicking a tattoo on the keyboard, Link considered what he might say next. His mind was full of questions, but the twist of her pretty features told him he did not want them answered right here or right now.

Without another word, Link turned and retraced his steps down the hallway. He heard a door slam behind him, and Link winced; when he glanced back, it only confirmed what he already knew. Sherry's office was the only one on either side of the hall that did not have the door propped wide open. He kept walking, and wondering.

Back at his desk, Link opened up his company email account. A slew of messages awaited him, just as he had expected. Most of them were announcements copied to everyone in his department, or everyone in the company; they always said the same things, in different words, and he deleted them without more than a glance. Only one message was addressed exclusively to him, from human resources. Link was sure it was a tally of his sick hours, or instructions on how to claim the ones he had used. After deleting all the others, Link opened it.

'Mister Nash,' it read. 'Human resources has received a potentially disturbing report from one of your co-workers concerning your behavior at work. Please note that we have scheduled a meeting with you on Thursday, January 5th at 10AM. Your attendance is mandatory.'

Link's heart was pounding in his chest, and he had to read the message three times over before digesting its contents completely. The rest of the email told him not to discuss the situation with anyone at work prior to the appointment, at risk of immediate termination. That should be easy enough, considering he had no idea what situation was up for discussion. Had he said something offensive to Steve, without knowing? Or had Sherry been so upset about him ditching the party that she had manufactured some story to get him in trouble?

They were the only two people he had run into, and both of them had acted like he had something they didn't want to catch. Link hardly knew anyone else in the office; if he was going to be completely honest with himself, he hardly knew Sherry or Steve either. When he opened his calendar, the appointment was indeed already scheduled for him.

His morning bubble had burst, and Link spent the remainder of the day and most of his spinning thoughts frantically wondering what was going on. The mistakes he had made earlier in the morning slipped his mind entirely, and were submitted along with the rest of his work minutes before the day ended.

THIRTY

Without stopping to eat or shower or even undress, Link headed straight for his bedroom as soon as he got home. He took two of the pills, collapsed on top of the comforter, and closed his eyes. Link wasn't quite sure if he felt the problems of many outweighed his own, or if it was just the best way to forget that he had troubles of his own; and he didn't care.

The robot Cervice had occupied was beyond cautionary measures. As soon as Link stepped into the room, the clumsy metal mechanism trundled out to meet him. Long awkward appendages sprouted from its sides, and it began speaking before he came to a halt before it.

"Are you ready?" Cervice demanded. "You had better be ready. I heard talk during mealtime today of an impending attack. Tonight. We must stop them."

Link nodded.

"I'm ready," he said.

He checked the firearm, although he had patted it a thousand times while traversing the corridor to the cafeteria. After patting it once more, Link pulled the pistol slowly from its holster. He held it in front of him, and gestured to the door.

"I'll cover you," he said.

The robot trundled forward slightly, then halted.

"Go ahead," it said. "I'll follow you."

Smiling, Link moved toward the exit. He looked both ways down the hallway, and motioned to Cervice.

"Come on," he said. "It's clear."

The corridors were deserted, and Link was surprised to see the entrance to the main deck open as they approached. He had expected a password, or a guard, or something.

Immediately after the wall reformed behind them, two other entrances appeared at opposite ends of the room. Link stepped back, shielding Cervice with his body, as he saw uniformed guards spill from the sudden openings. The door behind them remained sealed shut.

"It's a trap!" he hissed.

"It's not a trap," Cervice snapped mechanically. "It's what we expected. It's why you have a weapon. Now is not the time for hesitation, Link. Now is the time to do what you came here to do."

Link nodded resolutely, and brought the pistol up to eye level. When the sights lined up on a guard, he pulled the trigger.

This moment had been rehearsed in his mind so many times, Link expected to hear Cervice exclaiming at his skill as he swiveled smoothly to line up the sights on the next guard. He squeezed the trigger again, and finally noticed.

Nothing happened. Nothing had happened the first time he had pulled the trigger, and nothing happened this time either. Link swiveled again, back to the man he thought he had already shot, and squeezed the trigger one more time.

They were upon him before he could try again, and Link felt the pain as the body he inhabited was taken down onto the hard deck. He was pulled to his feet almost immediately, and he felt his hands being bound behind his back.

"Stop this!" he cried. "Let me loose! I'm The Admiral!"

The guard holding him chuckled, and called out to another.

"Hey, Rit!" he said. "Since when does The Admiral refer to himself in the third person, or go down so easy?"

Another man was attaching some kind of electronic leash to the robot Cervice was inhabiting. He looked up, and smiled.

"He doesn't," he said. "But don't trust aberrant behavior to tip you off when he comes back. I've never seen The Admiral jump for joy before, but he's likely to when he sees that his trap worked. Look who I've got here. I believe it's Cervice himself, the turncoat who tried to kill us all."

Link shook his head adamantly. He spoke at the same time as Cervice, emotion straining his voice while the robot spoke in a dull monotone.

"I told you it was a trap!" Link cried.

"You couldn't pull the trigger, could you?" Cervice asked.

Struggling against restraints that gave up nothing, Link frowned down at the ungrateful hunk of metal.

"I pulled the trigger!" he shouted. "Nothing happened!"

The guards holding them exchanged a knowing look, and pulled them both toward the giant screen that showed the fleet more than it did space. Another sentry approached the screen, and tapped it lightly with one finger. A menu of options appeared, superimposed over the space scene, and he chose one with another tap of a single finger. A large square took shape before them, covering an even larger portion of the view. The Admiral appeared in the image within it. He was smiling humorlessly, frozen in a single moment until the guard tapped the screen again. Before he did, the man leaned in toward Link and spoke.

"The Admiral knew you were coming," he said. "He has a message for both of you."

He tapped the screen, and the picture came to two dimensional life.

"Link," he said. "Hello. You still think you can defeat me?"

The Admiral paused, and seemed to look right at him.

"How adorable," he said.

Most of the time Link had spent peering out through The Admiral's eyes had not been time spent looking in a mirror. Link had watched through both the lenses of the other man's eyes and his consciousness, without ever taking special note of how much he and the other man resembled each other. Watching The Admiral speak gave him a strange kind of deja vu; it was like watching himself in a mirror, with different mannerisms and thicker muscles. He even marveled at how the other man must have told the guards to position them after they were captured; when he turned, it seemed he was clearly addressing Cervice.

"And you," he said. "You should have known better, old friend. You barely stood a chance against me one on one, in a battle of wits. Sending a moronic proxy was a mistake. It was also an insult to my intelligence."

"Hey!" Link cried, forgetting it was a recording for a moment.

Hearing his voice come out of his own face to insult him was very disconcerting. Nonetheless, Link hushed when Cervice shushed him.

"You designed an EMF generator that inhabited a ship of its own," The Admiral continued. "You clearly stated in your notes that you felt the proximity of the original generator to many of the ships was causing the memory difficulties, and that its location on the command ship was creating the most extreme problems in those on board. Instead of sharing this information you kept it to yourself, until you could use it to somehow gain complete control of the fleet. We took your plans, and built the new generator. You no longer have access to the EMF generator, even if you were free to roam this ship. It is difficult to determine your biggest betrayal, but these secret plans leave no question as to your motives."

The Admiral looked back and forth between them, his eyes settling once more on the robot as he took up his recorded monologue.

"And yet," he went on, "I am prepared to be generous to both of you. I have a special surprise for you in particular, Cervice. The main reason we knew you were on board was because we found your discarded body in a storeroom. I couldn't believe you would have the audacity to create an artificial body that looked like your old natural one, or the vanity to leave it behind for me to find; but there it was. Rather than destroy it, I kept it for you. While these men wait for me to regain control of my body, they will download your consciousness back into the vessel that looks so much like you did when you were still an actual person."

The Admiral leaned in, and seemed to glower at the robot.

"I can watch you," he said, "while you watch me destroy them all. And then, I can tear you apart with my bare hands. And that will be the end of it, finally. That will be the end of you. All of you."

Link felt his eyes going wide while he spoke; when The Admiral turned his way, he backed up instinctively. Rather than actually retreat, Link bumped into the man holding him and was pushed right back to where he had been standing.

"Link," he said. "You never had it in you to beat me. I don't blame you for not realizing that; Cervice should have given you that insight. The only surprise I have for you in this world is the pistol I swapped out for a dummy. When you get back to your world you will discover that I have been meddling in your life as surely as you have been meddling in mine, if you haven't realized it already. Let me assure you that it could be much worse. If you come back here again, you will long for something so simple as an affair you can't remember and a job you're about to lose."

Straining against whatever was clamped about his wrists, Link lunged at the guard holding him.

"Let me go!" he cried. "I'm The Admiral, dammit! Let me go!"

The man held him firm, and whispered fiercely in his ear.

"Is that Cervice, then?" he asked. "Have we captured our enemy at last, sir? Can we begin to savor the taste of victory?"

Link glanced down at the robot, realizing what an unlikely scene this was for these men. They may have lived alongside artificial life forms that looked nearly indistinguishable from them their whole lives, but one person's mind inside another's body was still new to them. He realized they were doubtful, under their bravado.

"That's a cafeteria robot," he scoffed. "And I'm The Admiral. Let me go immediately, and get this robot back to its station before mealtime."

They exchanged another glance, this time a questioning one. The guard at the controlling end of Cervice's electronic tether raised an eyebrow, and leaned in close to Link.

"Alright, Admiral," he said. "What's the passphrase?"

Link felt his eyes go to the robot, unbidden. He looked

away immediately, and tried to stare down the guard doing the asking. Rather than wilt under his glare, the man began to visibly gain confidence. He squared his shoulders, cocked his head suspiciously to the side, and knitted his brows together. Link tried to keep from glancing at Cervice again, and failed.

"Cervice is in our midst," he muttered.

Everything seemed to be happening all at once then. Cervice was doing the best version of shouting at Link that it could, asking him why he would say something like that. The guard holding Link began to handle him even more roughly, and hauled him to one side of the room while Cervice's captor wheeled the robot toward the other. Link tried to explain, calling out that it had been the passcode a couple days ago; he wasn't giving Cervice up to the enemy, he was trying to save the fleet.

With both of them shouting at the same time, neither of them heard what the other had to say. Link was taken through one opening while Cervice disappeared through another. He could do nothing but struggle and keep shouting, so he struggled and kept shouting.

THIRTY ONE

His heart pounding in his own chest, Link sat up in bed abruptly. He rubbed at his wrists, compulsively, and glanced at the bottle of pills on his nightstand. Next his eyes went to the digital display on his alarm clock, and he did sleepy math in his head as he unscrewed the lid from the bottle. He should have time to go back in, perhaps at just the right moment, and make one last attempt to help Cervice.

As the pills took hold he remembered The Admiral's words, and his warning. Suddenly everything made sense, or was at least starting to. He wondered what the other man had done with his life and his job, until his consciousness wandered to another mind entirely.

Link was strapped to a chair, facing the giant screen filled with fleet ships. Cervice was beside him. The robot was in the body his students had fashioned for him, and he looked especially human as he gazed at the floating assemblage. The cords binding Cervice were different than the ones wrapped about Link; they glowed with a quiet electrical current, and seemed to keep him immobile from the neck down.

Guards were milling about, each of them bent to some task. Link couldn't believe they were ignoring the two of them so completely; he leaned toward Cervice, and spoke in hushed tones.

"It's me, Link," he whispered. "What do you need me to do?"

Cervice continued gazing at the silent spectacle for so long Link suspected he might not have heard. He leaned closer, and opened his mouth once more to speak.

"Nice try, Admiral," Cervice spat, cutting him off. "You know as well as I do that nothing can be done at this point. Link is not coming back, and I won't survive the night. You can do away with the gloating, and leave me here alone to watch your madness cause consequences of epic proportions. Watch me watch it, if you want; but leave me to my own thoughts."

Link shook his head.

"It's really me, Cervice," he said. "I came back."

The robot turned slightly, and caught Link's eye. He shook his head, and went back to gazing sadly at the screen.

"It's of no consequence," he said. "The last of your attack ships are moving into position, and they won't have a very long window before my people figure out what they're doing and move on. I don't imagine you'll let that window of opportunity slip by. Get out of your chair. Conduct your orchestra of murder. Leave me be."

A soldier glanced their way, raised an eyebrow.

"Sir?" he called out. "Have we lost you again?"

Link shook his head, set his jaw.

"No," he said. "These restraints are getting uncomfortable. Let me out of this seat."

The man laughed.

"I'm sorry, sir," he said. "Your specific orders were to keep you restrained until the attack is over."

Link glared at him.

"I have to use the restroom," he said.

The soldier shrugged.

"You said you might say that, sir," he said. "You instructed me on what to say, if you did."

Straining against the cord that bound him as much as he could, Link continued to try to intimidate him with his fierce stare.

"Say it, then," he spat.

Glancing around to see if anyone else was hearing the exchange, the soldier shrugged again.

"Go ahead and shit your pants," he said. "Sir."

Link almost wished he did have to go, just so he could stink up the command center and strike back somehow. Instead he sunk back into his chair, and sighed.

"Sorry, Cervice," he muttered.

The robot turned his head, as much as he could, and frowned.

"Link?" he said. "It's really you, isn't it?"

Link sighed once more, this time in exasperation.

"Yeah," he said. "It's me. Fat lot of good that does us."

A low sound began to emanate from the robot's throat. At first Link thought he was coughing on something, and trying to keep it quiet; then he realized Cervice was laughing, a low rolling chuckle that he wanted only Link to hear.

"It's not over," Cervice said, still chuckling. "When the attack ships are in firing positions, there will be a delay before the order is given. All of the ships must check in and verify readiness, and in the time it takes them to do so my people will strike."

Link felt the blood drain out of his face as Cervice's eyes narrowed. He held Link's gaze, and went on.

"The field generated by this ship was not dangerous to anyone," he said. "It was neither too powerful for those close to it nor too weak for those far away. It was also not powerful enough to cover the entire fleet. The notes The

Admiral found were falsified, based on a problem I was forced to solve before we began this journey. At first, I thought we would need a giant unmanned EMF generator kept at a safe distance from the fleet. With a big enough field, the entire fleet could always remain easily within the ideal range. But this posed too many problems, and I hit upon another solution instead."

Cervice was still watching his eyes, and Link was doing his best not to let them glass over while the robot spoke. He must have been doing a terrible job, because the robot laughed. This time, it was with humor.

"It really is you," he said. "You couldn't care less."

Link opened his mouth, to protest; Cervice sighed, and went on.

"It's fine," he said. "I'll keep it simple. The notes The Admiral found were faked, as were the unmanned EMF generator plans he built."

Now he was even more confused; rather than say so, Link looked at the robot helplessly.

"You drew up fake plans for a generator?" he said.

The robot shook his head.

"No," he said. "The plans were real, but they're really just duplicating the system we have now. It's a generator that tunes into the frequency the other engines in the fleet run at, and bounces the signal off the hulls. No matter how big the fleet is, the signal stays consistent by using the other ships as repeaters. One unit generates the signal, but the fleet as a whole creates and sustains the field."

Link raised an eyebrow.

"I'm sure it's quite brilliant," he said, dryly. "But what's the point? How does making him build another generator do anything at all?"

Cervice was smiling again, and once more there was

no humor in the expression. He let his eyes wander back to the screen.

"With no one on board," he said, "my people can destroy it. We are unable to kill, due to our inherent programming; even the back door I opened only allows for defensive measures to be taken. However, we are not restricted from destroying inanimate objects."

This time the chuckle sounded darker. If Link had been forced to put a name to the sound, he may have called it evil.

"They're almost in position," Cervice said, his eyes still on the screen. "You better get going. I can't say with any certainty that you will not be affected by the field generator being destroyed."

Link looked at the robot, and tried to keep from shouting.

"Are you kidding me?" he hissed. "What's going to happen to me?"

Cervice frowned, his attention on the fleet.

"Could be anything, really," he responded. "You might be wiped clean. Your consciousness might be set forever adrift, unable to find its way back to your body. Even I am at a loss to scientifically describe how you came here in the first place, or repeatedly thereafter. I can't say what may happen to you. As I said, you should go. Let's hope this plan works."

Straining at the cords that bound him once more, Link saw a soldier approaching them. He whispered, in the moments he had.

"What plan?" he said. "Your plan to erase everyone?"

The man was standing in front of them before Cervice could respond, if he had meant to.

"Admiral," the soldier said. "The ships are checking in. We will commence attacking when the last one has reported their position and is ready to fire. It should only be a few minutes more."

Link strained against the cords until it hurt.

"Stop!" he cried. "Call them off! Tell them to retreat!"

Now Cervice turned to look at him; he ignored the soldier, who was also watching him carefully.

"You said you might say that as well, sir," the uniformed man noted. "Our instructions are to proceed as planned."

He began to turn away, and stopped.

"Whoever you are," he added, "you don't deserve to see this. The Admiral does. I hope you have a life of your own, and that you pay for this in that life a dozen times over."

The sentry shot a disgusted look at Cervice, turned and walked away. The robot ignored him, his eyes still on Link.

"You didn't tell him," Cervice said.

Link shook his head, and stared out into space like the robot had done only a minute earlier. He saw something drifting toward them, a small irregular object that was slowly growing larger as it got closer. It also became easier to make out what it was. Naked and frozen, the pilot had obviously had more time floating in space alive than Link thought he might. His stance was that of a soldier, legs straight and shoulders back. One arm was frozen forever at his side, the other was held to his forehead in an eternal salute.

Once he realized what it was, Link tried to look away. He found that he couldn't. He watched the stiffened corpse drift closer, until it collided silently with the ship. The saluting arm broke off with the impact, and the pieces floated away in two different directions.

The scene was filled with light suddenly, and colored lasers leapt into existence between a dozen ships and one oddly shaped craft in the center of them all. Link couldn't tell where the lasers came from, they appeared so quickly. Only the resulting explosion gave away the source, as a giant bright light soundlessly covered the screen.

THIRTY TWO

For a long and uncomfortable moment, Link stared blankly around his own bedroom. All he could remember was a bright explosion, and a world full of light. As far as he knew, the fleet was destroyed or dispersed in one way or another. The spacious lightness in his mind was surely a letting go of some kind, and he would have to spend the rest of his life wondering. Maybe the fleet had been real, maybe he had done his best to save them, and maybe some or all of them were still alive in some form.

Or maybe he had made it all up, an elaborate story where he could be the hero while his real life spiraled out of control.

Thinking of his real life brought Link firmly into the moment, and he checked the bedside clock to see just what moment it actually was. He shot out of bed, and went rifling through his dresser. Apparently his laundry had suffered along with everything else, and Link was forced to put on the least dirty outfit he could find lying on the bedroom floor. He splashed water on his face, ran some toothpaste over his teeth, and wetted his hair where it was most mussed. The coffee maker got a longing look from him as he passed it, but he knew there was no time to brew a cup.

Blowing through a couple stop signs and one red light, Link knocked on the door only five minutes after the appointment had called for him to be there. It opened a crack, and a woman he had never seen before looked him up and down through the narrow slit without saying a word. She opened the door a little more, still blocking his entrance.

"Mister Nash," she said. "You're late."

Link nodded.

"I know," he said. "I'm sorry. I—"

"Wait there," she cut him off. "I'll call you in."

The door closed again, and Link stepped back. He stood awkwardly in the hallway, looking one way and then the other without really seeing anything at all. When his phone rang, he nearly jumped out of his skin. Link fished the device from his pocket, and silenced it immediately. The screen told him what number was calling, and Link knew it wouldn't be a long call. He answered, held the phone to his face.

"Hello?" he said.

A woman's voice came back, clipped and concise.

"Mister Nash," she said, "this is Doctor Thresh's office. Please hold for the doctor."

Link shook his head, remembered she couldn't see him.

"I've only got a minute," he protested.

The line went quiet; then there was a click, and yet another voice speaking his name like it was a dirty word.

"Mister Nash," she said. "This is Doctor Thresh. You do realize, of course, that any prescription you get from another doctor will be brought to my attention."

Pulling the phone away from his face for a second, Link gave it a brief incredulous look. For a moment he let himself wonder if there had ever really been a time when addressing a man by his surname actually came off sounding respectful. He moved the device back to his cheek.

"Uh," he said, "hello to you too, Doctor. Someone in your office made a mistake, I'm afraid. I have not been to see any other doctor in years. I only have the one prescription, from you. I figured that's what you were calling about, and I'd really like the chance to talk to you about-"

"Mister Nash," she interrupted. "All prescriptions are logged in a database. Don't bother lying to me. I know you were having trouble sleeping. If the prescription I gave you wasn't working, you should have come to me if you wanted to try something else. The sleeping pills you are taking do not interact well with the prescription I wrote for you."

Link frowned.

"I'm telling you," he said. "I'm not taking anything but what you gave me. And I wasn't having trouble sleeping. Your database has it wrong. I am glad you called, though. I do have some questions about..."

As the door he was waiting on opened, Link trailed off. He could see into the room now, and catching a glimpse of both Sherry and Steve in the office threw him off guard a little. The woman holding the door was the same one that had told him to wait. Only one other person was in the office, and she was a stranger to him as well.

"Sorry, Doctor," he said into the phone. "I've got to go."

Link hung up, slid his phone in his pocket and followed the woman into her office. Steve and Sherry were seated, as was the woman he had never seen before. Four chairs had been lined up facing the simple desk; Link took the only available seat while the woman who had called him in moved behind her desk and sat as well. She let her eyes travel over all four of them, and settled at last on Link.

"Mister Nash," she said. "You can call me Missus Rucker. I'm sure you know why we're all here."

Frowning, Link tried to look around. He had taken the seat furthest from the door, next to Steve. Beside Steve was Sherry, and next to her was the woman he didn't recognize. All three of them looked upset, but Sherry and Steve both met his eyes at least. The other woman stared straight ahead, her face stiffened into a brave rigid mask.

Link sat back, met Rucker's eyes over her desk.

"Actually," he said. "I don't know why we're here. I think I might know what's going on, though. See, I've been taking a—"

"Mister Nash," she cut him off. "Is this your phone number?"

While she read off the familiar digits, Link wished he could tell everyone to stop calling him that already. He considered calling her by name, and imitating her tone; then thought better of it.

Link nodded.

"Yeah," he said. "That's my wireless number. But that's what I'm trying to say. I—"

"Mister Nash," she snapped. "Did you or did you not send explicit photographs to Miss Snell?"

Link looked around.

"Who?" he said.

The woman in the chair furthest from him dropped her mask, and turned in her seat.

"Me, Link," she said. "Haley Snell. Don't act like you don't remember me. I still have your disgusting pictures on my phone."

Her head fell forward, and her shoulders started shaking.

"He was being so nice," she choked. "I didn't see the harm in giving him my number. As soon as he got it, he started sending suggestive texts."

Haley lifted her head, for long enough to look over the desk to Rucker and over at Sherry. She went on.

"I...I knew he was with Sherry," she said, "so I told him to back off. I told him she was not a smart person to offend, since she is my boss and his. Also, I don't like cheaters."

When she lifted her head this time, it was to glare at him. Haley wiped away her tears, and pointed across Sherry at Link.

"That's when he started sending pictures," she hissed.

Link's head was spinning. He shook it, and it didn't help. Looking helplessly between the woman behind the desk and the one accusing him of something he couldn't remember, he shook his head again.

"What pictures?" he said.

Haley leapt to her feet, and glared down at him.

"You know damn well what pictures!" she cried. "Stop playing dumb! It isn't going to work! What you did was wrong!"

Putting his hands up defensively, Link frowned.

"Listen," he said. "That's what I've been trying to tell you. I really don't know what-"

"Mister Nash." Rucker slammed her hand on the desk. "You need to calm down. This is a serious offense, you are clearly guilty, and I don't appreciate your attitude."

Link let his hands fall into his lap. He looked around helplessly.

"I need to calm down?" he asked. "I'm not the one yelling. I'm just trying to explain. I've been taking a prescription that—"

"Enough, Mister Nash," she snapped. "Given the awkward nature of this situation, I have had to question your manager at length about the nature of your relationship."

He felt Sherry's eyes on him, and Link turned to her.

"You mean Sherry?" he said. "I barely know her. Honestly, I didn't even know she was my boss until a minute ago."

Sherry stiffened in her chair, and leaned across Steve to glare at him. Her face was a twisted mixture of anger and hurt.

"Seriously, Link?" she said. "Are you serious right now? You like to call me 'boss lady' when we…"

Trailing off, Sherry let her eyes and her shoulders drop.

"Again," Rucker said. "This is an awkward situation, and a very sensitive one. I was honestly hoping that seeing the way your coworkers feel about you would compel you to tender your resignation. Miss Snell has agreed to refrain from pursuing this further, so long as you do so. If not, I will need to run this further up the ladder."

The thoughts were spinning so rapidly through his head that Link was beginning to feel dizzy. He looked around the room once more, and finally noticed Steve avoiding his eyes like all the others.

"What about him?" he said. "Why is Steve even here?"

Steve looked at him now, shaking his head while holding his gaze.

"I wish I wasn't," he said. "I told you not to take those pictures, and I told you not to send them. But you did it anyway, while I was in the same cubicle. That made me very uncomfortable, Link."

Link felt the dizzy feeling in his head sink to his belly, and he suddenly felt nauseous. He stood up, and swept the room with his eyes one last time.

"I think I'm going to be sick," he said. "I have to go."

He barely heard the voice of the human resources woman calling after him, as he slammed the door shut behind him.

"You are suspended until further notice," she cried. "Don't come back unless we ask you to."

Lurching up the hallway, Link felt a little better with each step. By the time he reached the restroom door the feeling had passed. He walked by it and his cubicle without pause, and headed out to his vehicle.

THIRTY THREE

The feeling started as soon as he settled behind the wheel. Link wondered, as he keyed the ignition, if there was some way The Admiral had slipped the noose once more. Miles ticked by, and each one brought with it another set of memories about the man that looked so much like him somewhere out there in the universe. The Admiral had thought circles around him so many times, it was not long before Link was convincing himself the other man had done so again. By the time he pulled into his designated parking space, Link could not have been more certain.

He dashed up the steps to his apartment, slamming the door behind him as he jogged through his tiny living room. The bottle of pills was right where he had left it, and Link seized it and spun the lid off. Shaking it into his open palm, he watched five of them form a small pile in his hand. Link moved slightly, to dump a few back in; one of the pills tumbled to the floor with the motion, and he didn't bother to bend and pick it up. He had another look at the four remaining pills in his hand, shrugged and tossed them all in his mouth.

Settling his weight on top of the comforter, Link sighed as he closed his eyes. The last thought he had before his mind drifted away was that he might be setting it adrift forever. If he hadn't been lying down, Link surely would have shrugged again.

The shift was sudden, and shocking; Link felt himself tingling inside another man's body, tingling with the sensation of being the other man.

An armed soldier stood next to Link, and Cervice was on the other side of him. The robot was still bound by the electronic tether that limited his motion, and his eyes were locked on the enormous screen the same as the sentry beside him. Link was looking down, at his hands: they were free. He glanced at the armed guard, sidled up closer to him, and reached out quietly to slip the man's pistol from the holster on his hip. Before the other man could register the movement, Link was aiming his own weapon at his head.

"Set him free," Link said, jerking his chin at Cervice.

The robot peeled his attention from the screen at last, and looked up at him. Link grinned, without taking his eyes from the sights.

"Untie him," he snapped.

The guard frowned, and slapped his hand against his empty holster. Another uniformed man looked up from his task, and reached for his firearm as well. Link swiveled, shot the other man in the chest before he could draw, and lined the sights up on the first man once more. The soldier shook his head, forcefully.

"No," he said. "I won't do it. Go ahead and shoot me."

Link shrugged, and reversed the pistol. Placing the barrel firmly against his own temple, he arched an eyebrow at the man.

"How about now?" he said.

Immediately, the guard moved forward and knelt before the robot. A few others had noticed the skirmish, and were advancing with guns drawn. Link turned a slow circle, showing them the gun at his head and shouting at them.

"Go ahead!" he cried. "Shoot me! Or come one step closer, and I'll shoot myself! It won't hurt me at all, but it will kill The Admiral! Come on! Test me! Go ahead!"

Cervice was standing beside him at this point, and he leaned in close while the guard that had set him free backed away with his hands up.

"What are you doing, you fool?" Cervice hissed. "Pull the trigger!"

Still turning a slow threatening circle, Link spoke in a hushed voice from the corner of his mouth.

"I'm trying," he whispered. "I've been trying this whole time."

Link saw the robot's eyes go wide, until he turned so Link couldn't see him any longer. With his back squarely to Cervice, Link felt the robot reach out and grasp his arm.

"Come on," Cervice said. "This way."

Following the robot's lead, Link kept the gun to his head as he backed away from the troops. He caught a glimpse of the screen at last, and it was nothing but laser fire and scattered explosions. Debris filled the entire area. Between the floating bits of fragmented ships and the blinding light of the lasers, it was impossible to tell how many crafts remained. He glanced back at Cervice, and called to him over his shoulder.

"They're fighting!" he cried. "How are they fighting?"

The robot's voice came back, quiet and strained while pulling him.

"Some of the ships have the latest generation in command," he said. "Once they were attacked, they were able to start defending themselves. They aren't fighting so much as they are covering the others while they escape."

Still backing up, Link called out again.

"Won't that erase them?" he cried. "Why would they do that?"

Cervice pulled, and answered.

"Better alive and lost," the robot said, "than dead and forgotten."

Link kept his eyes on the soldiers, finally understanding why so few of them were paying attention to the skirmish. Each of them was bent to some task, firing at the enemy or taking evasive action. Only guards were engaging them, and all they were doing was watching them back away. One of them must have realized where they were going, and cried out.

"Stop them!" he shouted. "They're heading for the generator room!"

More sentries turned from their tasks, drew their weapons and started in their direction. Link had a chance to sneak another look at the screen. Still alive in sudden bursts of brilliant light that disappeared as soon as they formed, the section of space he was looking at was little more than broken pieces and explosions that threw more broken pieces in every direction. He saw a few ships streak away, but they were hard to track. One moment they were there, the next the screen filled with light, and the next there were less ships to see. It was hard to tell how many were getting away and how many were being destroyed. Clearly, the occupants of the escaping ships felt the same way as Cervice about existing in a diminished state rather than no longer existing at all.

Link lowered the weapon and reversed it. Still backing up, he began to take wild unaimed shots in the general direction of the converging troops. A couple went down, but most of his blasts struck walls or work stations. He followed Cervice through an opening as it formed, and backed into the room with his sights lined up on the open doorway.

Glancing around, Link saw placards spaced at regular intervals on every wall. Some were in words, others were pictures. Each of them bore the same message: firearms were not to be discharged in this area under any circumstances. Link hesitated as a uniformed body blocked the opening, and waved the gun at one of the posted warnings.

"Don't shoot!" he said, grinning wickedly. "See the signs?"

The guard raised his pistol, and fired. Streaking between them, the laser hit the floor and left a smoking pit at their feet.

"Get behind me!" Link cried.

He angled himself between the robot and their assailant, as another shot went wide and scorched the wall. Cervice grabbed his arm once more, and pulled him toward the metal where it was still smoking. The robot splayed Link's fingers apart for him and placed his palm over an access panel. An opening appeared in the wall, and the room was suddenly awash in engine noise.

Everything slowed down then, and Link watched the guard lift his pistol and take careful aim. He tried to move between them, but Cervice still had ahold of his arm. The robot sidled up close to the opening in the wall, and tossed Link bodily away from him. Link had no time to be amazed at the robot's strength, or brace himself before he hit. As his shoulder struck the floor, he rolled awkwardly and watched his pistol clatter away out of his reach.

The guard was shooting, no longer afraid of hitting The Admiral. All around Cervice, smoking pockmarks were taking shape in the floor and the wall. Link crawled toward his lost firearm, unable to take his eyes off the robot as he stood there unmoving. Now it seemed everything was moving at normal speed except him, and Link knew suddenly that he would not reach the weapon in time. He watched a shot take Cervice in the shoulder, and saw the robot collapse into the open panel. Link cried out, just as the guard took careful aim once more.

His cry was drowned out by another, as a soldier stepped up behind the one firing.

"Stop shooting!" he yelled. "He has the EMF generator panel open! Stop shooting, man! You'll erase us all!"

The soldier's brain had already registered the command to pull the trigger. Link watched his eyes go wide, as if he understood what was about to happen and couldn't stop it. A laser shot out of the barrel, and the entire panel filled with light. Cervice fell from the hole, one shoulder a charred stump and half of his face a twisted melted mess. Flames licked the wall all around the panel, and Link's reaching hand finally fell on the weapon he had dropped.

Link took one last look at Cervice. The robot was gone, but that didn't mean Link was not clear on what he had to do. He raised the pistol, lined up the sights on the blazing opening, and pulled the trigger repeatedly. The fire turned to a smoking inferno with the first few shots, as the guards raced across the room to leap on him. Before they could seize him, Link bit his lip and fired one last shot into the open panel.

The room was filled with a blinding light, a deafening explosion threw all three men against the far wall, and Link felt his consciousness slipping away as he struck the unforgiving vertical surface.

EPILOGUE

Her hand curled into a loose fist, Sherry knocked on the door for the third time. Several seconds passed with no response. She leaned into the jamb, called out quietly.

"Link!" she said. "Link, it's me. It's Sherry. Open up."

Again, she rapped her knuckles on the thin barrier.

"Link!" she cried, louder. "I saw your car! I know you're in there! Open up! We need to talk!"

Another stretch of silence was the only response. Sherry bit her lip, and tried the door handle. It turned in her hand, and she paused. Looking around, Sherry shrugged and pushed the door open slowly.

"Link!" she called out. "I'm coming in!"

The living room was no more or less a mess than she expected it to be. Sherry moved through the space, and hesitated before moving through the next door. It stood slightly ajar.

"Link?"

Her voice was barely a whisper at this point, although it sounded thunderous to her in the stillness before and after she spoke. Pressing on, she reached out and opened the door the rest of the way.

Sherry gasped, and rushed to kneel next to the bed. Link was lying on his back, his head propped slightly forward by a pillow. His jaw was slack, his mouth gaped open, and his lips were dry and cracked. Open and unseeing, his eyes gazed at nothing with a complete lack of intensity.

Waving her hand in front of his face, Sherry called his name again. Nothing roused him, even when she shook him lightly and then not so lightly by the shoulder. She tried to close his eyes, so she would stop being drawn to that awful empty stare. They popped open again immediately, as soon as she moved her fingers from his eyelids. Finally she stood up, and pulled her phone out of her purse.

The voice on the other end was terse, and insistent.

"Nine one one," she said. "Is this an emergency?"

Sherry looked down, shuddered.

"Yeah," she said. "My boy...uh, my friend seems to have had some kind of seizure, or stroke or something. He's totally unresponsive."

Quick and dry, the voice came back almost immediately.

"Were you taking drugs?" she asked.

Sherry looked around.

"I wasn't," she said. "He might have been. I only just got here. There is a bottle of pills on his nightstand. I've been texting and calling him for two days. He went kind of off the rails the last couple weeks, and really started turning into a completely different person. Of course, I didn't know him that well be—"

"What is your location?" the woman said, cutting her off.

Again, Sherry cast about the room with her eyes.

"Let me grab a piece of mail, or something," she said.

The next few minutes seemed interminable to her, and Sherry quickly tired of going over the scant details she could give over and over again. She realized the woman was just keeping her on the phone when she heard a knock coming from the other room.

"Oh!" Sherry said. "Did you send someone?"

"I did," she responded. "Are they there?"

Sherry nodded.

"Yeah," she said. "I think so. I'm going to check now."

Two paramedics stood waiting on the landing, a man and a woman; Sherry ushered them inside. She pointed to the open bedroom door, and spoke to the dispatcher at the same time.

"It's them," she said. "Thank you."

Without hearing whatever the woman might have said in response, Sherry hung up and trailed them into the bedroom.

"Thanks for coming," she said. "He was like this when I found him."

While the man leaned over Link's unresponsive form and tried to rouse him in much the same ways Sherry had only minutes earlier, the woman began to echo the dispatcher's string of questions.

"Does your boyfriend do drugs?" she said.

Sherry shook her head.

"No," she said. "I mean, I don't know. He's not my boyfriend. There are some pills, over there."

First she pointed, then Sherry moved to pick up the bottle. She untwisted the cap, and peered inside.

"It's nearly empty," she said.

She looked at the date, shook her head.

"This prescription isn't very old," she said. "It shouldn't be so empty."

The man had stopped trying to rouse Link. He looked up at Sherry, from his bent position, and jerked his chin toward his partner.

"Give those to her," he said. "You shouldn't be handling them."

Sherry frowned, capped the bottle again and passed it to the woman. They exchanged a glance, while the other paramedic put his attention back on Link; Sherry gestured toward the door.

"Maybe we should leave him to his work," Sherry suggested.

He jerked his head up, and looked at each of them in turn.

"I mean, thank you," Sherry smiled sweetly. "I just don't want to be in your way. Do you want a cup of coffee, or something?"

The paramedic shook his head, pulled a stethoscope from his pocket and clipped it about his neck.

"Your boyfriend seems to be in real trouble here," he said.

Sherry held her hands up in front of her.

"He's not my boyfriend," she said. "We were dating, for a minute; then he started acting weird, and kind of unbearable. Could it have been those pills? Do they cause erratic behavior?"

He was staring at her, the look on his face nearly as blank and uninterested as the one Link wore. The pills had gone into the woman's pocket, without either of them looking at the bottle. After a moment he shrugged, and looked away. He said nothing.

Sherry nodded.

"So," she said. "No coffee then."

She smiled weakly at the woman, and slipped from the room.

While she warmed up the machine and washed one of the several dirty mugs laying about the apartment, Sherry tried to listen to them through the open doorway. She could only pick out snippets of the conversation, most of which meant nothing to her. All she really made out clearly was him telling her they needed to go get the stretcher, and bring the patient in to be looked at. Sherry moved to the coffee brewer, and busied herself making a cup.

By the time they returned with the trundling cot, Sherry had found some creamer in the fridge and dumped a generous amount in her coffee. She noted that it tasted a little off, and checked the expiration date on the bottle. Sniffing the steaming brew, she could swear it smelled like a handful of coins were in the cup along with the coffee and flavored cream. Sherry shrugged, and had another long sip; she needed it, and the metallic aftertaste wasn't strong enough to deter her from drinking more.

The woman stepped into the room, walking backward. She was pulling the gurney, or guiding it; Link's feet came through the doorway first, followed by the rest of him. He looked as he had on his own bed, completely intact and absolutely absent all at the same time.

"You can't ride with us," she said, "unless you're family. Sorry. You can follow us, though. We're taking him to Western Memorial."

She looked apologetic, and Sherry couldn't figure out if it was because they couldn't give her a ride or because Link had become some kind of vegetable. Sherry nearly reminded them that he wasn't her boyfriend once more, though no one had suggested it for awhile. Instead she smiled, and nodded.

"Thank you," she said. "I'll be along shortly."

They closed the door behind them, and Sherry spoke aloud to the empty living room.

"Or not," she said. "Probably not."

Sherry yawned, and took her cup of coffee in the bedroom. She set the mug on the nightstand, next to Link's alarm clock. The pills were gone, as she assumed they would be; she wished she had at least written down the name on the bottle, so she could do a little curious research. Casting about with her gaze, she saw something on the floor next to the bed. She knelt to pick it up.

Pinching it between her thumb and forefinger, Sherry brought the single pill up close to her face and inspected it carefully. Before regaining her feet, she noticed something she hadn't seen while she had been standing. She reached under the bed, and fished out another bottle of pills. The label said they were some kind of sleeping pills, and the prescription date was even more recent than the other had been. She opened the bottle, and peered inside.

A distinct metallic odor wafted from the bottle. Sherry crinkled her nose at the smell, and glanced at the coffee cup she had set on the nightstand. She reached out, picked it up, and compared the odors. Exhaustion had fallen over her like a wet blanket, and she was pretty sure she knew why. She yawned, as if to illustrate the point, and set the coffee and the pill down next to each other.

Taking her phone out of her purse once more, Sherry opened the camera app and took a photo of the pill. She dusted it off against her blouse, made sure the photo was clear, and popped it in her mouth.

Sherry lay down, and closed her eyes.

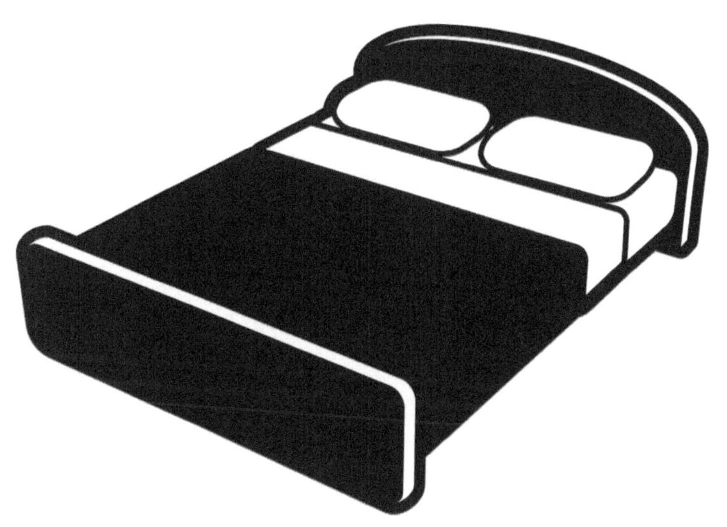